D1625280

Rawhide Robinson Rides the Range

RAWHIDE ROBINSON RIDES THE RANGE

TRUE ADVENTURES OF BRAVERY AND DARING IN THE WILD WEST

ROD MILLER

FIVE STAR
A part of Gale, Cengage Learning

GALE
CENGAGE Learning®

Detroit • New York • San Francisco • New Haven, Conn • Waterville, Maine • London

GALE
CENGAGE Learning·

LIBRARY OF CONGRESS CATALOGING-IN-PUBLICATION DATA

Miller, Rod, 1952–
    Rawhide Robinson rides the range : true adventures of bravery and daring in the wild west / Rod Miller. — First Edition.
        pages cm
    ISBN-13: 978-1-4328-2802-8 (hardcover)
    ISBN-10: 1-4328-2802-9 (hardcover)
    1. Cowboys—Fiction. I. Title.
PS3613.I55264R39 2014
813'.6—dc23   2013031783

First Edition. First Printing: January 2014
Find us on Facebook– https://www.facebook.com/FiveStarCengage
Visit our website– http://www.gale.cengage.com/fivestar/
Contact Five Star™ Publishing at FiveStar@cengage.com

Printed in Mexico
1 2 3 4 5 6 7 18 17 16 15 14

Rawhide Robinson Rides the Range

INTRODUCTION

Rawhide Robinson was an ordinary cowboy.

Unlike the legendary Pecos Bill or Breckinridge Elkins, he had no superhuman powers. He moved at an ordinary pace, rode ordinary horses, was born and raised in an ordinary family, wore ordinary cowboy garb; was, in all ways, totally ordinary in appearance and manner.

But extraordinary things happened to Rawhide Robinson, to hear him tell it.

And tell it he did. For if there was one way in which Rawhide Robinson departed from the ordinary, it was in his ability to talk. In fact, he seemed to lack, in all ways, the skill of silence. When riding herd, his voice could always be heard reciting poetry, rehashing soliloquies, singing songs, whistling, and otherwise holding forth for an audience of none (or one, if you counted himself; two, if you counted his mount; or hundreds or thousands, if you counted cattle).

Put him in a crowd—around the campfire with the crew, say, or in the bunkhouse on an evening, or propped against the bar in a saloon—and Rawhide Robinson irresistibly fell into performance mode. Rhyming verse, familiar and unfamiliar, rolled off his tongue in mass quantities. Inspiring speeches by characters from Shakespeare's plays. Bible verse of an entertaining nature.

But, mostly, Rawhide Robinson related tales of his own experiences, stories of his adventures wandering the Wild West as an ordinary cowboy.

Most folks appreciated his stories, listening in wide-eyed wonder (and, occasionally, jaws-agape fascination) to florid descriptions of danger and derring-do. Some (a sizeable minority, but a minority nonetheless) thought Rawhide Robinson a liar—a bloviator of the worst order, tending toward exaggeration at best and total fabrication at worst.

The truth about Rawhide Robinson and his cowboy adventures?

You decide.

CHAPTER ONE

In which Rawhide Robinson and a bogged steer visit Pikes Peak

It was back in the summer of aught-seventy-one, or eighty-three, or thereabouts. Rawhide Robinson was at the time an ordinary cowboy on an ordinary trail drive from the depths of Texas to the Kansas railheads, the most popular of which was, just then, located at Dodge City.

His days were ordinary for the time and place—he would arise from his bedroll before dawn, settle his wide-brimmed thirteen-gallon hat on his head, put on his pants one leg at a time, use the mule-ear straps to pull on high-heeled Texas Star boots with gal-leg spurs permanently strapped to the heels. A bacon-and-beans-and-biscuit breakfast, washed down with blistering hot coffee, was the ordinary breakfast fare.

Like any ordinary cowboy on a trail drive, Rawhide Robinson next hobbled over to the remuda in the rope corral and chose a mount. As the wrangler roped out his horse, Rawhide Robinson briskly rubbed warmth into his hands in anticipation of taking hold of a pair of bridle reins, the main tool of his trade, and riding out the brief bout of bucking, which was how an ordinary cow pony started the day.

Saddled up and mounted, as he would be until a brief dinner break around noontime, Rawhide Robinson rode to the herd, taking up his position as an ordinary rider on the flank. (Although long experience qualified Rawhide Robinson for duty farther up the line as a point rider or even as scout, he did not push the issue as he was happy working as an ordinary cowboy and, in fact, would have been happy riding drag.)

The day upon which we meet Rawhide Robinson was an ordinary one; hours of ambling at a relaxing pace across the prairie, occasionally galloping out from the herd to turn back a wandering beef but, mostly, Rawhide Robinson and the other hands rode along without incident. The day ended with a river crossing. Well, calling it a river overstates the case, but getting a herd across any stream can be trouble. But this day's fording was a piece of cake as the cattle walked calmly into the slow-moving water and out the other side without ever swimming a stroke.

With the cattle bedded, supper on the inside of the drovers, and sleep not yet upon them, it was time for a song, a poem, or a story to put the lid on the day and uncork the night.

And, whenever Rawhide Robinson was around, quiet would not likely last—a story wouldn't be long in coming.

The crew scattered around the campfire; some squatting on spurs, some sprawled on the sod, others propped against bedrolls, still others stretched supine on their sougans. Most of the hands were ordinary cowboys, their names not recorded and thus lost to history. The man in charge was Enos Atkins, trail boss. There was an experienced hand named Doak and a handy drover from the Arizona Strip country known, oddly enough, as Arizona.

And there was a cowboy barely past being a boy, name of McCarty, on his first drive. As with many boys rehearsing for the role of a man but unsure of the lines, McCarty was, at various times, hotheaded, softheaded, hardheaded, pigheaded, jugheaded, knuckleheaded, bullheaded, muddleheaded, blockheaded, chuckleheaded, boneheaded, thickheaded, dunderheaded, and downright difficult. But the youngster was extraordinarily accomplished in one area—he had mastered an extensive vocabulary of the profane variety. His catalogue of cuss words could make a preacher blush and melt the gilt edge off the pages of a Bible.

As was his custom, Rawhide Robinson unfurled his bedroll and sat upon it, back leaned against his saddle and feet to the fire. Sparks streamed into the sky like an upside-down rain shower as Enos Atkins stirred up the coals and tossed another skinny log on the campfire. "Say, Rawhide, this ain't your first trip up the trail, is it?" Enos said, knowing that with Rawhide Robinson, that one implied question would get the evening's entertainment rolling and keep it going into the wee hours.

"Oh, no," Rawhide replied. "I been up the trail with many a herd. Why, I followed a herd a lot like this one some years ago. We were bound for the railhead at Ellsworth, Kansas, with a sea of beeves belonging to Mr. Ford Fargo of the Double-F-Slash Ranch. Thing was, though, I never made it to Kansas, as misfortune set in along the way, as has often been the case with me."

Rawhide said no more, letting the statement lie there like an unbranded calf, knowing it was only a matter of time before one of the hands grabbed it.

"So, ^&#@$! What happened?" the young cowboy named McCarty blurted, ending the uncomfortable pause.

"Well, it was a crossing, like today," Rawhide Robinson said. "But we was crossing a particularly nasty river, the Canadian. And it was raining. I'll tell you, it was coming down like pitchforks and baby pigs. We was hurrying along, trying to get them cattle across before the water got too high. I was on the far bank soaked from the soles of my boots to the crease of my hat, keeping the critters bunched once they climbed out of the water, when this one old mossy horn bunch quitter started swimming upstream. I followed along with him, there on the bank, knowing he'd come ashore once he figured he was clear

11

of the herd and could make his getaway.

"Thing was, though, when he tried to get to dry land he got bogged. That river along there is awash in quicksand and that nasty old steer had found him some of it. So I punched a hole in my catch rope, figuring to land a loop around his horns and drag him out of there. It took me two tries, but I did manage to snake a long loop around his big old rack. He wasn't none too happy about that—snortin' and blowin' and bellerin' and wavin' them antlers around like he'd like nothing better than to poke one of them in my eye.

"But I started in to hauling him out of there just the same. Thing was, though, the lasso rope I was packing was an eighty-foot Mexican gut line, and you all know how a rawhide rope acts when it gets wet. That old horse and me kept pulling and that steer kept sinking and that reata kept stretching.

"Well, we just kept on pullin' and pullin' and pretty soon we was out of sight and out of earshot of the river, the herd, and that steer. Stretchin' and stretchin' we went, and before you know it, what with the rain and all, I lost all track of time and distance and just kept on ridin'.

"All of a sudden that rope went slack and before I even had time to realize that the steer had come unstuck, here he comes sailing through the sky and flies right over my head. Now, not being one of them California-type dally ropers, my reata was tied hard and fast to the saddle horn, so I figured there'd be trouble when that rope pulled tight.

"Thing was, though, that gut line was so soaking wet and stretchy there never was much of a jerk. When that steer hit the end, it just started stretching again, and soon enough it yanked that horse right off the ground and sent him a-sailin' through the sky. And, being firmly planted in the saddle at the time, I was along for the ride.

"We just kept swappin' ends, spinnin' around and around up

there like one of them bolo things them gauchos down in South America throws, and me not knowin' when it would ever end. After a while, the rain let up as we flew on beyond the storm, and soon the sky cleared and the sun started shining.

"I had no idea where we were or how much country we had flown over. Finally, though, I recognized the Rocky Mountains and noticed we was flyin' right toward Pikes Peak, way up there in that Colorado country. Well, we flew right past that steep and craggy old jaggedy old pointy old mountain peak, that steer on one side of it and me and the horse on the other. Then, as you might imagine, we reached the ends of the rope and started spinning around that mountain in opposite directions, with the rope wrapping around and around and around that peak tighter and tighter and tighter, just like some Californio taking his dallies.

"So when the rope finally ran out, we all—me and that horse and that steer—ended up clinging like spiders to a wall on the steep sides of that rocky peak wonderin' what to do next. Thing was, though, that rawhide rope was dryin' out fast, shrinkin' up around that mountaintop and squeezin' it tighter than a kid does an ice cream cone. Before you know it, that shrinkin' rope pinched the top right off that great big mountain. Squoze it plumb off and sent that peak rolling down the mountainside busting into ever-smaller pieces until it was all gone.

"And that ain't no lie."

"Rawhide Robinson, that's the biggest bunch of #*%!$^/ nonsense I ever heard in all my born days!" the young cowboy said.

"McCarty," Rawhide replied, "have you ever seen Pikes Peak?"

"No, I ain't. Never been outside of Texas as yet. What's that got to do with it?"

"Any of you boys ever seen that mountain?" Rawhide asked.

"I seen it," Enos, the trail boss, said.

"What's the top look like?"

"Well, it's big. A big ol' mountain. The top, well, it's just kind of bulgy and rounded, looks sort of smooth-like."

"It ain't all steep and jagged, with a big old pointy top?"

"No, Rawhide, it ain't."

"You see," Rawhide grinned. "It's just like I said! I done pinched the top of that mountain right off."

"&%@*#!" McCarty said. "Ain't no such thing."

" 'Tis so," said Rawhide. "And that ain't the half of it."

Enos asked, "Meaning what?"

"Well, what I found on top of that lopped-off mountaintop was something to set your head to spinnin'."

"What was that?" said McCarty.

"That," Rawhide Robinson said, stretching full length on his bedroll until the saddle became his pillow, then, sliding his wide-brim hat down over his face, "is a story for another day."

CHAPTER TWO

In which Rawhide Robinson teaches a young cowboy a lesson in proper manners

Rawhide Robinson enjoyed a few hours of uninterrupted sleep under the stars, oblivious to the snorts and snores of his sleeping saddle pals, before rolling out for his round of night guard, as ordinary cowboys did on a trail drive. As it happened, he shared the shift with McCarty, which led to a certain amount of discomfort as the young cowboy hurled insults Rawhide's way with each circle.

See, riding night guard amounted to nothing more than riding around and around the herd on a sure-footed horse listening—for one couldn't always see much in the dark—for trouble. From time to time thunder and lightning or varmints such as coyotes and lobo wolves and rustlers might upset the herd and cause a stampede, and the drovers on night guard were always on the lookout for such.

But, ordinarily, it was a lonesome job and a cowboy often spent his two hours in the saddle alone with his thoughts, except when his circle met the other night guard's round. The solitude suited Rawhide Robinson just fine, and he used the opportunity to brush up on his songs and poems, for it was well known amongst those who trailed herds that a cowboy's voice engaged in such recitations kept the cattle calm.

From this valley they say you are going, Rawhide Robinson crooned as he rode.

We will miss your bright eyes and sweet smile.
Just as he started in on the lines that go,
For they say you are taking the sunshine,
That has brightened our path for a while, he came to the part of the circle where he passed McCarty going the opposite direction.

"You're a dirty low-down)&#@&* liar, Rawhide Robinson," McCarty said as he rode past.

Come and sit by my side if you love me,
Do not hasten to bid me adieu, sang Rawhide, ignoring the impertinent young cowboy.

Just remember the Red River Valley,
And the cowboy who loved you so true.

"I don't intend to listen to any more of your #&%*@! lies," McCarty said on the next round.

Rawhide sang, *'Twas there that Annie Laurie gave me her promise true . . .*

While Rawhide Robinson feigned to ignore McCarty, he heard every word. The slurs continued when next they passed.

"I never heard such <?+#@* lies in all my born days," Mc-Carty said as Rawhide Robinson quoted Alfred Noyes:

> *He rose upright in the stirrups; he scarce could reach*
> *   her hand,*
> *But she loosened her hair i' the casement! His face*
> *   burnt like a brand*
> *As the black cascade of perfume came tumbling over*
> *   his breast;*
> *And he kissed its waves in the moonlight . . .*

When finally his turn at night guard ended, Rawhide Robinson rode back to the wagon for another short round of shut-eye before facing another day on the trail. He rolled out for breakfast in the ordinary way and stomached his biscuits and beans and cowboy coffee. McCarty happened to reach the washtub at the same time Rawhide dropped in his tin plate.

The youngster said, "You remember what I said, Robinson. I don't want no more of your *@&%# lies told around this camp."

"You know, McCarty, men have been killed for less than what you said. I've cut you some slack since you ain't much more than a button, but you better lay off."

"Or what?"

"Ordinarily, I'm a peaceful man," Rawhide Robinson said. "But you don't want to get me riled."

"Or what?" McCarty said again, shoving Rawhide Robinson away with both hands in the middle of his chest.

"I'm telling you to back off. And I won't tell you again."

The youngster balled his fists, ducked his head, and charged Rawhide like an angry bull. But Rawhide slipped McCarty's first punch, stepped easily to the side, and tripped the stubborn boy.

Rawhide was upon McCarty before he knew what hit him. With a knee in the small of the boy's back, he pulled a piggin' string—a short length of rope used for hog-tying cattle—from the waistband of his chaps, looped it around the youngster's ankles and pulled it tight. Next, he bent one of McCarty's arms behind his back, double-half-hitched the tail of the rope around the wrist, and pulled it tight, trussing the boy up as tidy as a calf for branding.

Trail boss Enos Atkins ran toward the ruckus and asked, "What's going on here?"

"Ain't nothin' out of the ordinary," Rawhide Robinson said. "This boy needed some advice on dealing with recalcitrant calves, so I gave him a little education."

"Well, I won't brook no nonsense in this here camp. First sign of trouble, some one of you will be walkin' back down the trail carrying his saddle on his back."

"Don't you worry none, Enos. I believe McCarty's learned his lesson."

"I hope so," the trail boss said as he walked away.

Rawhide Robinson unloosed his piggin' string and helped McCarty to his feet. The boy rubbed the blood back into his wrist with a look of anger shaded with embarrassment.

"You was lucky that time, old man."

"Lucky!?" Rawhide laughed. "Ain't no such thing. Why, I'll show you luck. I ever tell you about the time I rassled a badger in my bedroll up on the Powder River? Now *that* time I was lucky!"

"*&@#$!" McCarty harrumphed and stomped away.

Rawhide hollered, "Remind me to tell you about that some time. It'll surely curl your eyebrows!"

CHAPTER THREE

*In which Rawhide Robinson starts a gold rush and goes
prospecting, in that order*

Following the unfortunate incident with McCarty, Rawhide
Robinson rode out for another ordinary day on the cattle trail.
No stampedes. No rustlers. Not even a river crossing to upset
the routine.

So when, after another supper of bacon and beans and
biscuits, the hands spooled out their bedrolls around the
campfire, they were especially eager for a break in the monotony.
Which meant turning to Rawhide Robinson for a story.

"Say, Rawhide," the cowboy known as Doak said. "You was
saying something else happened up there around Pikes Peak.
You gonna tell us about it?"

"Oh, ^@+#%*!" McCarty objected. "No more of Robinson's nonsense! Please!"

Enos said, "You best mind your manners, McCarty, or you
might end up trussed up like a bawlin' calf again. Go ahead on,
Rawhide."

Rawhide Robinson rooted down onto his bedroll, pulled off
his boots and spurs, and leaned back against his saddle. "Now
then," he said. "Where was I? Oh, I recollect now. It was when
me and that steer ended up on top of Pikes Peak and my reata
pinched that peak plumb off. That right?"

"That's it," Doak said.

"*&@#+^&!" McCarty said.

"Hush up," Enos said.

"Well, anyways, we was sitting up there, me and that ol' steer," Rawhide Robinson said. "And I noticed that all around us on that brand new mountaintop was these big yellow hunks of what looked to me to be pure gold. With the sun goin' down, it was all sparkly and shiny and flashin' yellow light for miles in every direction. I'll tell you, it looked right pretty, glimmerin' like that in the sunset, sendin' off all them golden rays. The glow on that big ol' mountain must have been visible all the way to the Missouri River.

"Well, I gathered up what I could stuff in my saddlebags, then I sacked out for the night, figurin' I'd ride down off that mountain come morning and see how and where to stake me a mining claim."

And Rawhide Robinson talked on.

"Thing was, though, when I opened my eyes there was prospectors everywhere, crawling all over that new Pikes un-Peak like flies on a pasture flapjack. And there was so many claim stakes sticking out of that mountain it looked like a porcupine. Fact is, it reminded me of that one time I got all shot full of arrows on the Llano Estacado—but that's another story."

"Oh, dagnabbit Robinson, I ain't listening to another +?%#@* word of this!"

"What's the matter, McCarty," Rawhide Robinson asked, "ain't you never heard of the Llano Estacado?"

"No! I mean, yes! But that ain't what I'm talking about. I mean that other *%<@# stuff, about the gold."

"Oh, I see. What you mean is, you ain't never heard of the Colorado Gold Rush."

"Of course I have!" McCarty said.

"And didn't you ever hear that gold rush saying, 'Pikes Peak or Bust'?"

"Sure I did."

"See, McCarty," Rawhide grinned. "It's just like I told you!"

"★$(+/@%!"

"You two stop your arguing," Enos said. "McCarty, you just shut up and let Rawhide tell his story. Rawhide, you shut up and talk."

"Well, okay then. Like I was sayin', I got to talkin' to this one old prospector name of Sourdough Saleratus and he allowed as how all the good claims thereabouts was already taken. Too crowded for his taste, besides. But he said he knew of some promising terrain over in the Arizona Territory, and that if I'd use what gold I had gathered up, up there on Pikes Peak to grubstake us, he'd take me along and we'd be equal pards all the way, fifty-fifty.

"So I did and we did—we loaded up on supplies and such equipment as we'd need and me and old Sourdough Saleratus set out for Arizona Territory to strike it rich. It was one heck of a journey, I'm here to say.

"We made it through them Rocky Mountains after day after day of up and down, into canyons and over passes and across rivers and through gorges and down valleys. Why, there was places the sidehills was so steep the deer growed their legs longer on the downhill side just to keep from tipping over."

"That so?" asked a wide-eyed Doak.

"Sure as I'm sittin' here," Rawhide Robinson said.

"&#-/@$!" McCarty said.

"Shut up, McCarty," Enos said. "Tell it, Rawhide."

And Rawhide Robinson talked on.

"Now, where was I?" Rawhide Robinson wondered. "Oh, I remember. Anyways, we followed along this river called the Gunnison, which for some ways was down in this deep canyon. So deep it was, it never had a bottom. Why, you could drop a rock down there and you never could hear nor see it land. Thing was, besides being deep, that canyon was so narrow in some spots you could step across it. Darndest thing I ever did see, but I seen it."

"(@$*&#!" McCarty said.

"Hush up, McCarty," Doak said.

"Go ahead on, Rawhide," Enos said.

"So, anyways," Rawhide Robinson said, "sooner or later that river joined up with a bigger one, the Colorado, and wound its way into this red-rock country you wouldn't believe. Heck, I don't believe it and I saw it with my own eyes. Nothing but solid rock, for miles in every direction. Why, our horses and pack mules wore their hoofs plumb down to nubs walking on that sandstone days on end.

"Wound up, we had to cut little axles and wheels out of cedar trees and strap a set on each one of their legs, or we wouldn't never have made it. I'm tellin' you, we hadn't any choice— that rock ate up iron shoes like ice on a hot day. Them animals skated and scooted around unsteady for a while till they figured out how to travel on them wheels, but they soon enough figured it out.

"So, anyways, we followed that river for what seemed like forever through that desolate country. I don't see how anyone could ever live there, but folks did. Leastways they used to. We seen whole towns out there, built out of rocks and mud. Some of them clinging to cliffs so high all you could do was look up at them. Only thing we could figure was them folks that used to live there could fly like them cliff swallows, or bats."

"That so?" Doak said.

"That's so."

"That's +)%*#@!" McCarty said.

"Hush up," Enos said. "Go on, Rawhide."

"Well, it's true. We saw lots of them places. Crawled right in some of them we could get to. Wasn't nothing in most of them but dust, but in some places we saw these little shoes made out of some kind of grass, fancy baskets wove from willows and straw and such, clay pots painted with pretty designs, all manner of strange objects."

"$)?$#@+!*"

"Hush up!"

"Some places them people, whoever they was, drawed all these pictures, right on the rocks. Some of 'em, you could tell what they was, deer and antelope and bears and such. But lots of them was pictures of critters like I ain't never seen nor even heard tell of. Only thing me and Sourdough could think was they was monsters, and that's why them people run off and left—them creatures scared them plumb out of the country."

"Them creatures still out there? You see any of them?"

"I'll tell you, son, we heard 'em, most every night. Scared the daylights out of us. Kept our stock stirred up, too. Couldn't hardly sleep, we had the heebie-jeebies so bad."

"But did you see any?"

"Well, I reckon so. One night, way, way late it was, I woke up with a chill on account of our fire had burned down. Anyways, I wandered out of camp to hunt up some wood, just worked my way upstream in this old dry wash where we was. Was a full moon out that night, and them strange-lookin' rock formations cast even stranger-lookin' moon shadows.

"Anyways, I found a dead cedar tree that must have washed downstream in a flood and got itself lodged in some rocks. So there I was, bustin' off limbs, when I heard something behind me. Didn't hear it so much as felt it, I guess. Sort of like a hot breeze blowin' down the back of my neck.

"I turned around and there was this big, tall, hairy something standing right there. Sixteen feet tall if it was an inch. Foul-smelling yellow smoke was streaming out his snout, and his eyes glowed hot orangey-red, like coals in a blacksmith's forge."

Rawhide Robinson stopped his story right there, letting his saddle pals squirm with the tension. Finally, someone busted out with, "Well, what did you do?"

"I lets out a beller would've woke the dead, had there been any thereabouts. Must have startled that thing, whatever it was, on account of he jumped in the air about a hundred feet and lit atop a rock pinnacle. I didn't waste no time hot-footin' it back toward camp, I'll tell you. All along I could hear him up there leaping from rock to rock to rock, like it weren't nothing. Just when I thought I was gonna make it to camp, that thing dropped out of the sky and lit in front of me on all fours."

"What happened? How'd you get away?"

"Well, boys, I'm sorry to say, I didn't."

"What!? What happened?"

"Why, that monster ripped me limb from limb and chawed on my bones like they was roasted spare ribs. If I hadn't already been killed, his gnawing on my carcass like that would have scared me plumb to death."

After a few seconds of shocked silence, the cowboys cut loose with hearty laughter, save McCarty. With a "~%#@=+*!" he started for Rawhide Robinson with balled fists and bristling neck hair. But he hadn't taken but two or three steps when Enos stuck out a booted foot and tripped him up. The young cowboy fell headlong, then sat up spitting fire and dust.

"Calm down, boy. Ain't nothing but a joke."

"&>$@^/! I'll get him yet! I just can't stand his lies!"

"Take a walk, McCarty," Enos said. "Cool off that hot head of yours, and don't come back till you remember your manners."

"%(=+/*!" he said, stomping off into the darkness.

"So, Rawhide, I guess you never did make it to Arizona to hunt for gold," a curious cowboy said.

"Oh, sure I did. Once I recovered from my unfortunate

demise, me and ol' Sourdough Saleratus went on our way along down the Colorado River and soon enough got to the place he was lookin' for. I gotta admit, though, I don't know how he knew we had got there, as that country is devoid of landmarks as anyplace I've seen—and I've seen a lot of places.

"That Arizona Territory is some kind of country. Not much water to be found, except what thin mud runs in the river, and about the only thing that grows good is rocks. Why, there's whole mountains made out of just one boulder. And ground so hard I doubt a herd of stampeding elephants would leave a trail. And me and Sourdough Saleratus set in to prospecting, plumb out in the middle of all that desolation."

And Rawhide talked on.

"I'll tell you, boys, I never worked so hard in all my born days. I'd dig and dig and dig on the banks of that river and that old man Sourdough Saleratus would wash and wash and wash that dirt with his gold pan, expectin' every shovelful to show color. But it didn't, and so we'd start over again. I'd pick and I'd shovel and ol' Sourdough'd swish and he'd swish that pan and eyeball every speck of every shovelful I dug up.

"Thing was, though, he never did see what he was looking for. We never found a trace of any minerals whatsoever. No gold. No silver. No copper. No nothing. All me and Sourdough Saleratus got for all our work was a big ol' hole in the ground. You can still see it, if you care to, and that ain't no lie. Any of you boys ever hear of the Grand Canyon?"

"That's plumb crazy, Rawhide! It just can't be so."

"Ain't you seen it, Doak?" Rawhide asked.

"No, I ain't seen it. And you ain't neither, if you ask me. Why, I'll bet a dollar and a drink at the end of the trail that there ain't none of us has seen the Grand Canyon—including you, Rawhide Robinson."

"You lose, Doak—I done been to the Grand Canyon myself,"

the quiet cowboy called Arizona said. "I come from that country, you know."

"Well, tell them what it looks like, then!" Rawhide said.

"Oh, it's big. That sucker stretches for miles. And not only is it long, it's wide. And deep. And it's got all these other canyons hooked into it, ever' one of 'em deeper than anything you ever saw.

"And if you look way, way down in the bottom from some places up there on the edge, you can see that there's a stream down there. Looks like a little bitty old creek, but they tell me it's a great big old river. Biggest hole in the ground I ever saw, that Grand Canyon."

Said Doak, "Well I'll be darned!"

"See fellers," Rawhide Robinson said as he stretched out full length on his bedroll and plopped his hat over his smile. "I wouldn't lie to you."

"{&@=#<*!" McCarty mumbled as he trudged back to the fire and sagged onto his sougans.

"#%)–%+ . . ."

CHAPTER FOUR

In which Rawhide Robinson single-handedly turns back a wild stampede

Clouds boiled up over the western horizon all afternoon and the wind whipped across the prairie, pushing a haze of dust ahead of the coming storm. As evening fell, Enos ordered all hands to mount a fresh horse, make do with coffee and cold biscuits for supper, and stay in the saddle.

"This weather's got these beeves stirred up," he said. "There's likely to be lightning, and that could put 'em on the run. You boys best be ready to ride."

Rawhide Robinson called out his most reliable night horse from the remuda. A sharp-eyed, sure-footed horse with a calm disposition was a valuable asset on any night, and a priceless partner in a stampede. He tucked half a dozen biscuits into the pockets of his India rubber slicker, stretched his cinches snug, swung into the saddle, screwed his hat down tight, and rode out to the herd.

The rain started soon after, making the cattle reluctant to bed down. Instinct told them to turn tail to the storm and drift along with the wind. Unfortunately, that would take the herd at right angles to the drive's intended direction of travel. The drovers kept constant pressure on the steers, turning back onto the bed ground any that attempted to wander. Unwilling to lie down and relax, the animals were up and down, up and down, nervously stirring all through the night, never more than a lightning bolt away from running.

Fortunately for the cowboys, the lightning stayed distant and the rolling thunder was never loud enough to panic the herd into stampeding. Still and all, it was a long, miserable night for steers, horses, and cowboys alike. The cook managed to get a smoky fire going, and when dawn finally grayed the sky, the cowboys gulped down gallons of strong coffee topped off with fresh biscuits and reheated beans.

But there was no rest. Enos ordered the cowboys to push the jumpy herd northward, knowing from experience that trail fatigue would soon enough take the edge off their inclination to bolt. The day proved a short one, however. They pushed the cattle hard for three or four hours, covering enough country to reach the next river crossing. The rain-swollen stream proved too high to ford so the cowboys bedded down the herd and settled into camp for some much-needed rest.

Little was heard around the campfire through the afternoon, save a lot of snoring. Come evening, the hands pitched into an ordinary meal of beans, bacon, and biscuits with a vengeance, and topped off the meal with a rare cook's reward of dried-apple cobbler.

"Well, boys, we dodged a bullet last night," Enos said as they relaxed around the campfire. "A stampede ain't nothin' to sneeze at, I'll tell you. Hard on the herd, and can be death on a cowboy. We lucked out."

"Ain't that the truth," Rawhide Robinson added. "You don't never want to be in on no stampede."

"I guess you'd know, eh, Robinson?" McCarty sneered.

"I reckon so. Why, there was this one time—"

"No way," McCarty interrupted. "I ain't in no mood for another one of your *!&#+@% stories."

"You just hush. I wanna hear it," Doak said

"Yeah, me too," another cowboy said.

"Tell it, Rawhide."

And so Rawhide Robinson settled into his story.

"I joined on with a crew contracted to drive a big herd of Mormon cattle out of Utah Territory to California, where beef was on the menu for all them gold miners there. Them Saints gathered stock from all their settlements and drove them to Utah Valley, just through a gap in the mountains a ways south of Salt Lake City.

"Had probably five, six thousand head there waiting. The plan was, see, to divide them up into two or three herds of manageable size and set out one by one on the southern trail to California to avoid them high passes in the Sierra, on account of it being fall, when travel on the Humboldt and Overland trails gets iffy.

"So, anyways, we had all these cattle just bidin' their time there. Like it is in that Great Basin country, we were in a long, narrow valley between two mountain ranges. Thirty some miles long, I guess, maybe half that much wide.

"You'd think being that close to all them little Mormon towns we could of got some decent grub, but that sure weren't the case. Cook for that outfit was about the sorriest excuse for a dough puncher I ever did see. Everything he fixed either needed more salt or was so salty it dried you out so bad you couldn't quench it with a gallon of coffee.

"And his biscuits. Land sakes, sometimes they's so soft in the middle you could stretch a bite half a mile. But, more often than not, they was dry and hard as a pine knot. More than a few of the hands in that camp was whistlin' their esses on account of breaking off teeth trying to eat them biscuits."

"^#*&#@!"

"Shut up, McCarty."

"Tell it, Rawhide."

"Well, as it turned out, them biscuits saved the day."

"How's that?" a cowboy asked.

"I'll get to that," Rawhide said. "Just hold your horses. As bad luck would have it, one evening a big storm rolled into there through them mountains and before you know it, it was streamin' down rain, wind blowin' it every which way, lightning crackin' the air and thunder like to knock a man right out of the saddle. I happened to be ridin' circle when the worst of it hit.

"And I'm here to tell you boys, seein' six thousand steers hoist their tails and head for the high country is a sight to behold. Their poundin' hooves and rattlin' horns was enough to drown out the sounds of that storm. The ground was shakin' like there was a whole herd of railroad trains rollin' through there.

"Anyways, try as we might, we couldn't do nothin' but try to keep up with them cows. My night horse had lots of bottom, and slow but sure we inched our way up to the front of that herd. But it didn't do no good. I hollered, waved my slicker, whapped their noses with my reata, and shot my pistol plumb empty and them leaders kept right on runnin' like I wasn't even there.

"I had just about given up when I remembered I had a greasy sack of them rock-hard biscuits slung to my saddle horn. So I started flinging them biscuits at the leaders of that stampeding herd, and I tell you, them steers took notice. Knocked two or three head plumb to their knees, made many another change direction."

"(&+@$#!"

"Hush!"

"Soon enough, I got them turned with them flyin' hunks of crust and eventually got that big herd to milling. There bein' so many cattle in that herd it was a mighty big circle, but once I got them turning, we just kept them milling around and around and around the middle of that valley. All them poundin' hooves made a heck of a mess—wore a muddy boghole in that ground that kept on getting deeper and deeper and deeper. Then that hole started filling up with rainwater and runoff from the storm and before you know it, we had to push them beeves onto higher ground just to keep them from drowning.

"Next morning, when the clouds cleared and the sun came up, there, in the middle of that valley, was as pretty a lake as you'd ever want to see."

"Lake?" McCarty said. "You mean mud puddle."

"No, I mean *lake*. Twelve, fifteen miles long, five miles across, twenty feet deep or thereabouts, it was, in spots—still is, for that matter. You look on any map of that Territory, and you'll see it, just like I said. Utah Lake, they call it."

"&*@#!=>! Next thing you know, you'll be tellin' us you filled the oceans!"

"No McCarty, I never done no such thing. And if I didn't do it, I won't tell it 'cause everything I'm tellin' you boys is God's honest truth. I never filled no ocean. . . .

"But I did cross one horseback one time, come to think of it. You mind your manners, McCarty, and I'll tell you about it someday," Rawhide Robinson said as he covered his face with his Stetson hat and settled in for a good night's sleep.

CHAPTER FIVE

*In which Rawhide Robinson invents an essential item
of cowboy regalia*

The storm that delayed the herd's river crossing must have been a big one upstream, for the stream was still running too fast and too high the next morning to risk a passage. So, other than taking their turn riding guard around the herd, the cowboys stayed in camp.

They checked their saddles over carefully for wear and tear and repaired what needed fixing, stretched the kinks out of lariats, aired out bedrolls, washed and dried socks, greased wagon wheels, trimmed hooves, and performed whatever odd jobs came to hand.

But the crew spent most of the time lazing around; filling up on coffee and enjoying the rare opportunity for much-needed rest.

Rawhide Robinson, from his usual perch atop his bedroll, leaned back against his saddle, steaming tin cup of coffee in hand, surveyed the situation. He watched the cowboy called Arizona brush the mud from his batwing chaps and tighten the whang leather laces.

"That's a fine-looking pair of chaps you got there, Arizona."

And they were. Made of tough but soft tanned leather, a row of three shiny silver conchos along the thighs reinforced the snaps and straps that held them in place. A buckle, also fashioned from Mexican silver and etched with a fancy design, decorated the waistband. Most impressive of all was the silhouette of a tall saguaro cactus, cut from green-dyed leather and neatly stitched to each batwing.

"Why, thank you, Rawhide. I'm mighty proud of these *chaparreras*. Custom made by a Mexican saddle maker way down in Agua Prieta. Mighty fine work, if I do say so myself."

"You know, I actually invented chaps," Rawhide Robinson said. "I ever tell you boys about that?"

"%(<*@! Not again!"

"Hush up, McCarty. I wanna hear this," a cowboy said as he refilled his coffee cup. "Talk on, Rawhide. Tell us."

Rawhide Robinson moseyed over to the campfire, tipped the outsized coffee pot hanging on its swivel hook from a tripod over the coals, and refilled his tin cup.

"There was this time I was out in California," Rawhide said once he'd settled back into his nest atop his bedroll. "It was right after we delivered that herd of Mormon cattle I told you about. Anyways, I didn't have nothing on after that job so I was just bumming around, riding the grubline, giving that country a look-see.

"And I'm here to tell you boys, it's something to see. Just about any kind of place you're looking for will be found out in California. They got big, fertile valleys growing grass faster than cows can crop it off, mountains as steep and rocky as they come. They got forests and deserts, lakes and streams. And, of course, there's that ocean out there—remind me to tell you sometime about how I rode across that ocean horseback."

"C'mon, Robinson, get on with it," McCarty said. "If we gotta listen your &=#@%*(nonsense, let's get it over with so's I can get some rest."

"Keep your shirt on, boy. It's my story and I'll tell it in my own good time. So, anyways . . . now, where was I? Oh, right. I was just bummin' around out there in California. They got these huge ranches out there, where the Spanish has been rais-ing cattle for a long, long time. Had all these Mexican and Indian cowboys punchin' them cows, and they had their own way of doing things. *Vaqueros,* they call 'em. Or Californios.

"Where we'll just cinch a saddle to a colt and ride out the storm till he's broke, they'll spend weeks calmin' them down. Why, they ride 'em in a hackamore for a while, then shove a spade bit the size of a dinner plate in their mouth but don't hardly touch the reins. Them horses'll do anything, almost without asking. Cut cattle out of a bunch, run 'em down for roping, keep a herd movin' along, work 'em in pens. It's a sight to see.

"And talk about roping. Why, most all them boys twirl skinny little rawhide ropes that must be eighty, ninety feet long. They don't ever tie off, but dally up around the saddle horn and never lose anything they catch.

"And they can catch anything. I'm telling you, they can pitch a loop from any direction—overhand, underhand, sidearm, backwards; they can rope the head, the horns, front legs, hind hocks. I swear, them loops have eyes of their own. Them vaqueros can throw a rope around a blind corner and dab a loop on whatever's hiding there."

"@>?^*#!"

"Hush up, McCarty."

"It's the truth, I'm tellin' you," Rawhide Robinson said. "Why, time was, California was overrun with grizzly bears. But they ain't many left anymore on account of them cowboys wore them all out roping them. They say they'd put on bear-roping exhibitions in city parks."

"?($@&<!"

"It's the honest truth, I'm tellin' you. But, them vaqueros didn't run off all them grizzly bears, which brings me to my story."

"Finally."

"Pipe down, McCarty."

"Talk on, Rawhide."

"Well, here's the thing. Up on the western slopes of them Sierra Nevada mountains out there, they got piney-like trees taller than you can imagine. You can stand at the bottom of one and look up and the top's so far up there it plumb disappears into the clouds.

"They're thick as ticks on a hound dog's back on them slopes, but they thin out on the ridge tops on account of the wind up there's so stiff it peels the bark and needles right off 'em and, often as not, tips over any tree that gets more'n an inch or two tall. But, there's still a few tall ones up high there, ones tough enough and limber enough to hang on in that wind.

"I'm ashamed to say how this story starts, boys, but the fact is I was afoot in them mountains one afternoon. See, this green-broke colt I was ridin' bolted when a rattlesnake started in to whirrin' its tail and before I could get him whoa'd up, he run under a tree and scraped me off on a low-hanging limb.

"Hit the ground like a sack of mashed potatoes, I did. I was padded up pretty good, as it was just coming on spring at the time and still a mite chilly in the mornings. Had me on a Mackinaw coat and two pairs of wooly socks, pair of duck trousers with a pair of buckskin britches over the top of them.

"So, my landing was soft, as them things go, but, still and all, it took me a few minutes to get my breathing apparatus to workin' again. Then I set out through the trees after that horse, tryin' to follow the racket of cracking limbs and busting rocks and ripping saddle leather.

"I was gaining on that hammer-headed colt when the woods opened up into this pretty little meadow. As luck would have it, there was an old sow grizzly bear nosin' around out in that little park. Must have had a cub or two nearabouts, 'cause she sure didn't cotton to me and that pony being in the neighborhood. She lit out after us; me being behind that colt made me the primary target.

"So we's movin' at top speed when we hit the trees, headin' for the high country. Thing was, nobody ever told me that uphill is a bear's best direction, and there ain't no way you can outrun one."

"^%+@?#! Don't tell me you got ate by that there bear!"

"Don't be daft, McCarty. Had she killed and ate me I wouldn't be here to tell this story."

"Shut up, you two," Enos said. "Quit your quibblin'. Tell it, Rawhide."

"Well, anyways, I was gaining on that horse every step, but that sow bear was gaining on me even faster. Got so close I could feel the heat of her breath on the back of my ears.

"Lucky for me, I came to this big ol' tree and set into climbing. Just before I got out of reach, though, that bear bit the seat plumb out of them buckskin britches I was wearing—feeling that cool breeze on my backside spurred me on, I'll tell you.

"Fortunately, a full-grown grizzly bear ain't much of a climber, so I figured if I got high enough I'd be safe and could just wait her out. So I climbed way up in that tree and sat me down on a limb and wrapped myself around that tree and settled in for the duration.

"Which idea would have worked out just fine had the wind not kicked up about then. That big old tree started in to swaying in that wind, back and forth, back and forth, back and forth, getting closer and closer to the ground on either side with each arc.

"Well, that bear saw she could just about get to me on the low ends of those swings, and was there to meet me at the bottom of every one. She'd stand up on her hind legs and reach out for me with them paws the size of frying pans, decorated with claws as long as a Bowie knife.

"Them razor-sharp claws ripped a slit in them buckskin pants from the knees on down, which, lucky for me, was as high up as she could reach. But she kept after me, and them claws soon enough had the bottom ends of them buckskins shredded into fringes as nice as you like. So there I was, wearin' my cloth trousers under them leather britches, which, thanks to that grizzly bear, had no seat, was split up the sides, and all fringed on the edges.

"And that, boys, is how I came to invent the chaps all cowboys wear nowadays."

"Robinson, that ain't nothing more than more of your ⋆=!%&# nonsense," McCarty said, the only one of the hands not laughing.

When finally he got his breath, Arizona said, "Rawhide, I never knowed that's how chaps was invented and I'm mighty pleased to know the truth of it. But what happened next? You can't just leave us hanging with that bear still on your tail!"

Rawhide refilled his coffee cup then settled in to finish the story.

"So there I was, boys, swaying back and forth in that pine tree with that big old sow grizzly bear swatting at me at every turn, and me not knowing whether to climb up or down. Well, I realized neither direction would do me any good so I had to figure out something else or I'd meet my demise by becoming bear breakfast.

"So, I unstrung my lasso rope from the saddle and started in to building a loop."

"Rope!? Saddle!? What the &⋆@!+?< you talking about? You're up a tree!"

"Well, sure, McCarty. Everyone knows that. Maybe I neglected to mention that horse had climbed that tree ahead of me, and was in the same fix I was in."

"@+(#*$&!"

"Now, don't get all up in a huff. I'm just telling you what happened."

"*#!>(+$!"

"Pipe down, McCarty. Let Rawhide tell his story. Talk on."

"Anyways, I managed to get a loop around that she-bear and pitched the slack over a limb. I mounted up and jumped that colt out of that tree to see if my plan would work. It did.

"When we went down, that grizzly, being at the other end of that rope, which was tied off on my saddle horn, went up. With us being on the ground and that bear being up the tree, I figured we was safe.

"Then my miscalculation occurred to me when I realized that even though we had switched places—we being on the ground and that bear up the tree—we was roped together and I wasn't going anywhere.

"I set in to thinkin' my way out of that one, which proved unnecessary as along about then that tree branch I'd slung my rope over decided to break off and that big ball of fur and fangs and claws and nasty attitude came tumblin' down on top of us. You wouldn't believe the ruckus. Sounded like a schoolroom full of kids, or a pack of dogs on the trail of a herd of wounded javelinas.

"Well, we finally got untangled and that colt hit the trail at a high lope with that bruin hot on its tail. I figured this time my goose was cooked, as I would never catch up to that horse, what with the bear urging it on. And, truth be told, by that time I wasn't sure I wanted anything more to do with that jug-headed colt nor that bear, neither one.

"So, anyways, I set out to walking down off them mountains, not looking forward to the trip, but having no alternative I could think of. There I am, hobblin' along downhill, threading my way through that thick jumble of trees and bushes on them hills when I hears this racket coming from up above. Limbs cracking, rocks rolling, trees falling—why, it sounded like a whole herd of elk was bearing down on me."

Rawhide Robinson rose from his bedroll and sauntered over to the cookfire to refill his cup once again. He took his own sweet time moseying back, letting his story slowly boil like the coffee in the pot. But the anticipation was more than Enos could stand, and when the steam started coming out his ears, he boiled over.

"Rawhide!" he hollered.

"Oh, sorry, boys. Got kind of lost in thought there. Where was I?"

Enos said, "You was walkin' down the mountain when you heard this ruckus."

"That's right. Let me see now," he said, taking a moment to scratch his bristly whiskers, eyebrows scrunched in thought. "Well, here's how it was. That commotion, whatever it was, just kept on a-comin'. I broke out into another of them little mountain meadows and was hoofing it across there quick as I could muster. Just when I got near to the other side, that noise came bustin' out of the trees behind me."

A sip of coffee stalled the story.

"Well?" said a cowboy.

"And?" said another.

"I hesitate to say what I saw, fellas. You ain't gonna believe it. I know I didn't believe it and I saw it," Rawhide Robinson said around another sip of cowboy coffee.

"Well?!" said a cowboy.

"And?!" said another.

"I looks behind me, and here come that colt out of the trees, on a beeline right for me. . . ."

"WELL!?" said a cowboy.

"AND!?" said another.

"Well, sittin' in the saddle, comfortable as if she was born there, was that she-bear, lariat in hand, spinning a loop pretty as you please—with me in her sights."

Most of the cowboys laughed.

"It's a true story, boys. You ever run across an old cowboy name of Sunny Hancock, just ask him. He tells it better'n I do!"

"!^@&#*$(!" McCarty hollered. ">&%*$#+!"

Rawhide Robinson smiled and sipped his coffee.

CHAPTER SIX

In which Rawhide Robinson rescues an unhorsed rider from
a raging river

Dawn found Enos Atkins on the riverbank. The trail boss studied the still-fast-moving water, wondering if a crossing was possible. Though down considerably from the day before, roiling waters still tumbled uprooted trees, limbs, and other debris downstream, adding danger to any attempt to reach the other side. But experience told him that cattle could cross if handled properly. Back at camp, he told the crew to fill up on breakfast for it was unlikely they'd see hot food again until evening.

"Boys," he said to the drovers once they were mounted and ready, "the river's still running hard, but I believe it's safe enough to cross. If you pay attention. This water ain't so deep that the beeves will have to swim much, if at all.

"But that water's movin' fast and it's carryin' all manner of trash, and the footing ain't all that good. So keep a leg on each side of your horse and your mind in the middle or you'll find yourself upset and swimmin'."

Rawhide Robinson knew Enos had it right. He'd seen many a swift-water crossing and knew the biggest danger was the unexpected. With his sure-footed night horse between his knees he expected no difficulty and hoped the other hands were likewise well mounted.

"Well, boys, we might as well get our feet wet," Enos said. "Let's get 'em up and on the move."

Whooping and whistling and hollering and shouting filled the air for hours as the cowboys kept the cattle strung out, pushing the herd into the river in a constant stream. Other than having to rope and drag the occasional steer that lost its footing, there were no mishaps to speak of.

Near the end of the day, with most of the cattle dripping on the far bank and the tail end of the herd in sight, the cowboys were spent, and fatigue took the edge off their attention. So it was with McCarty, the most inexperienced rider in the river. He didn't see the log in the water until it was upon the herd. It plowed into the side of a steer, rolling the animal under the muddy water. That set the log into a spin, knocking cattle out of the way in its relentless trip downstream.

As the steers tried to recover, McCarty kept prodding them, hollering and thrashing them with his coiled lariat. One of the steers had trouble regaining its feet and the cowboy leaned out of the saddle and grabbed a handful of tail to give the steer a lift.

The log hit as it rotated in the swift water on its next turn. The off-balance horse went down when the log swept his hind legs out from under him, and the thrashing animal rolled over the rider as it went down. McCarty managed to kick free of the stirrups, but with cattle knocking him to and fro in the roiling water, and weighed down by waterlogged boots, jeans, chaps, shirt, and vest, he was unable to find his feet.

He flogged around amid the frightened cattle, trying to keep his feet on the river bottom and his head above water, but a steer horn snagged his vest and spun him into the path of another animal that pushed him under and, struggling for the bank, trompled the cowboy underfoot.

Rawhide Robinson saw the whole thing as he worked the downstream side of the herd, nearly opposite where McCarty rode. He saw the young cowboy's hat pop to the surface and watched as his shirt floated up, ballooning with trapped air. Reining his horse around, he rode downstream through the stirrup-deep water until well clear of the herd, angling to intercept the floating cowboy. Building a loop in his waterlogged reata, he managed to pitch it over one of McCarty's arms as the cowboy rolled over and past in the rushing water.

Hauling in and coiling rope as quickly as he could, Rawhide reeled in his catch. Grabbing McCarty by the collar, he hoisted the waterlogged cowboy out of the river, draped him across the fork of his saddle, and rode for the shore, pounding the boy between the shoulder blades with the flat of his hand as he went. As the overloaded horse humped his way up the far bank, McCarty heaved a gout of water and drew a ragged breath. Rawhide again hoisted him by the collar, lowered him to the ground, and, satisfied the cowboy was breathing, turned and rode back into the stream.

Meanwhile, Arizona had retrieved McCarty's mount, which seemed no worse for wear, as the other hands kept the herd moving across the stream in good order despite the commotion. Rawhide pushed a few downstream wanderers back into the mainstream of the herd, riding back and forth through the rushing water to keep the cattle in line.

Finally, the stragglers struggled up the bank, shook water from soaked hides, and trotted uphill to where the herd was bedding down. Tired out from the crossing, the cattle would likely spend a quiet night. One by one, the cowboys rode into the camp, grateful the cook had coffee on and supper in the making.

McCarty huddled near the campfire, wrapped in a henskin—a lightweight feather-stuffed quilt from his bedroll—while his clothes hung on willow branches poked into the ground, drying in the breeze and the heat of the fire. Save for a couple of horses left saddled and staked out, readily accessible in an emergency, the cowboys pulled the kacks from their mounts, stood their saddles on end and draped saddle blankets over them to dry, and turned the horses loose to graze with the remuda.

Plopping down next to the fire, Rawhide Robinson squeaked off his boots and poured muddy water from them, peeled off holey socks and wrung them dry.

"You all right, McCarty?"

"I'm fine."

"Thought we'd lost you there for a minute," Enos said.

"I woulda made it," McCarty said, ruffling sand out of his drying hair. "That water was so thick with mud a feller couldn't hardly sink in it."

"Well, you sure did. Had Rawhide not pulled you out, we'd be pounding a wooden cross into the riverbank in your memory."

"@(+#%*!"

"What? You oughta be grateful, son. Not cussin' about bein' saved."

"Ah, don't bother the boy, Enos," Rawhide said. "I reckon he's a mite embarrassed. But there weren't nothing he could have done. Could have been any one of us. Why, I remember one time—"

"?<*$&#!"

Enos, on the edge of anger, said, "McCarty! What's your problem?"

The boy hung his head and mumbled, "I just don't want to end up in one of them %<{]@#*$ stories of Rawhide's, that's all."

CHAPTER SEVEN

In which Rawhide Robinson goes hungry and gets wet

Enjoying another ordinary evening on the trail, the cowboy crew settled in for rest and relaxation around a crackling fire, sipping coffee and feeling well fed and satisfied.

"Cookie surely does whip up a fine batch of apple cobbler," Doak said. "I swear, that stuff's even better today than it was yesterday when first made."

"That's true enough," someone agreed.

"It's right tasty, all right."

"Never had anything finer."

Someone else added to the conversation with a satisfied belch.

"What do you think, Rawhide?" Arizona asked. "You ever eat anything finer?"

"I'll tell you boys, I have enjoyed some mighty fine meals on the trail," Rawhide Robinson replied. "But, truth be told, I think it was more on account of hunger than the *haute cuisine.* When your belly button's bouncing off your backbone with every step your horse takes, darn near anything on any tin plate tastes mighty fine."

"Hot what?" McCarty said.

"Not hot, kid," Doak said. "It's *haute. Haute cuisine.* It means fancy grub. It's lingo from over there in France."

"Well, ^*@>?#! Why don't he just say so, then?"

"Whyn't you just hush up and pay attention. You just might learn something once in a while. That is, if anything can make

45

its way through that thick head of yours."

"Doak! McCarty!" Enos said. "You two knock off the chin wagging. So, Rawhide, what's the best thing you ever ate on a drive?"

Rawhide laughed. "I don't know as I ever ate anything much other than beans and bacon and biscuits. An occasional hunk of fried beef now and then, maybe, or a pot of son-of-a-gun stew. Once in a while, you get a treat like Cookie's apple cobbler.

"But, I'll tell you boys, like most ordinary cowboys, I been hungry a lot more often than I been fed. Why, I remember this one time—"

"Oh *#}=@%, not again!"

"Stuff it, McCarty," Doak said. "C'mon, Rawhide. Tell it."

"You boys recollect when I told you about that herd of Mormon cattle we took to California?"

"We heard it."

"And you remember about how I told you how the biscuits the cook on that crew made was so hard they could fell a mule if you hit it between the eyes with one?"

"We remember."

"And you remember how them biscuits did, as a matter of fact, knock down enough steers to turn back a stampede?"

"A lot of &+@#^* if you ask me."

"Nobody asked you, McCarty. Talk on, Rawhide."

Rawhide Robinson refilled his tin cup with scalding coffee, letting his audience stew for a few minutes as he gathered his thoughts. Finally, settling into his usual perch atop his bedroll, feet to the fire and back propped against his saddle, he slithered into his story like a bull snake down a gopher hole.

"Boys, let me tell you how bad the grub was on that trip. Eating that dough roller's beans was like about the same as chewing a mouthful of gravel. Why, they never was cooked enough to eat, hardly, and wouldn't have been worth eating if they had been. Nothing but beans boiled in river water. No salt, no bacon, no chili peppers, no nothing. Except for gas. Them beans had more air in them than the crew could get rid of, even working at it full time.

"I already told you about his biscuits. Then there was the coffee. Sakes alive, that stuff was thick and black as axle grease. You could float the lid off a Dutch oven in a cup of that stuff. And never mind stirrin' it. Bend a spoon double, if you even tried. Stuff didn't pour out of the pot as much as it plopped in glops.

"I'll say one thing for that coffee, though—it stayed hot. You could pour a cup of a Sunday morning and still be sippin' at it on Thursday. By Friday, maybe, you could drink it without scaldin' all the hair off your tongue. Would have come in handy, had it been winter. But we was travelin' across the hottest, driest darn desert in all creation.

"All in all, it was pretty sorry chuck. You never seen such an assembly of skinny cowboys. Had we not been wearin' our wide-brimmed hats, we'd have been downright invisible. Most days we was so scrawny we didn't even cast a shadow. I'll tell you, the one time it rained out in all that desolation on that drive some of the hands didn't even know it. We was all so narrow of frame by that time that the raindrops plumb missed us. The onliest ones of us got wet at all was them that was movin' around and chanced to walk into a raindrop or three."

">%&*#!"

"Pipe down, McCarty."

"But, like as I said, gettin' wet wasn't a problem because it only ever even thought about rainin' that one time. Things wasn't so bad for a while, as we kept pretty close to what they call rivers out there in that territory. Ain't hardly worth the name, though. There'd be a pretty good stream runnin', then it would turn into a trickle, and 'fore you know it there weren't nothin' but mud and pretty soon, dust. Then, a ways on downstream there'd be water again. Never could fathom where it went or where it come from.

"Then, we struck that Colorado River and followed along it for a while—you boys recollect me tellin' you about them diggings me and Sourdough Saleratus made prospecting on that river?"

">&#@%*!"

"Pipe down, McCarty," Doak said. "Sure we remember. Go on with it."

"Well, this was somewhere downstream from that place, and some years later, and I'll tell you boys, that stream was still runnin' more mud than water from where we stirred it up."

"*@+}%!"

"Hush up!"

"Well, it don't matter none, 'cause that story ain't got nothin' to do with this one," Rawhide Robinson said. "Pretty soon, we had to turn away from that river and then there weren't no water for miles. We finally got to a place called *Las Vegas,* which is the name them old Spaniards gave it, meaning 'the meadows.' So we rested there a day or two, fed up them steers, filled them up on water, and headed out into the desert again, toward California.

"Day after day we pushed those cattle, them bein' hungry and thirsty all the time and us the same. Alkali dust burnin' our eyes, sun bakin' our brains, and that dry air parching your lungs till you couldn't hardly get your breath. Hot as it was in the daytime, come night it got downright cold. And there weren't nothin' hardly to build a fire with, all except some scrawny little scraggly brush that burned up fast like tumbleweeds and didn't have a degree of heat in it.

"We tried trailin' them cattle in the daytime, we tried drivin' them at night, and soon enough we was doin' both; stopping

only when them steers'd start tippin' over from plumb tired-
ness. Then we'd rest awhile and hit the trail again, stirrin' up
that desert dust in the general direction of where we was goin'.

"Which trail wasn't that hard to follow, mind you—there was
plenty of bones and busted wagon wheels to mark the way, left
by other fools who'd gone before. When we did get to one of
them so-called water holes out in that desert, they was dry as
them bones. Even diggin' deep as we could we couldn't stir up
any mud, let alone water. But, we was in it and there weren't
nothing for it but to keep goin' till we got out of it.

"Came a night we stopped to rest, with every man and cow
among us wonderin' if that stop would be our last. Didn't hardly
dare close our eyes, fearing we wouldn't ever open them up
again. Finally, though I dropped off to sleep.

"Don't know why—maybe on account of I was so darn
thirsty—I dreamed I was in a rainstorm. Real gully washer, it
was, raindrops the size of dinner plates splashin' down
everywhere. Never seen such a storm, leastways not in real life.
But I sure did dream one up that night, I'll say. Swallowed so
much water I swelled up like a bloated heifer. Sad to say, when
I woke up it was every bit as dry in that desert as it had been
when I dozed off.

"All 'cept for one thing, that is," Rawhide Robinson said as
he ambled over to the cookfire to refill his coffee cup.

"Well, what was it?" Arizona asked.

Rawhide Robinson moseyed back over to his bedroll and
took his accustomed seat, blew the hot off his coffee, and took a
leisurely sip or two.

"Here's the thing. I picked up my boot and noticed it was a
mite heavier than it ought to've been. Thinking some critter had
crawled in there to keep warm, I tipped it over to give it a good
shake and—and this is the honest truth, boys—rainwater started
pouring out of that boot!"

McCarty busted loose with a "&#?*]@!" and kept up his ranting until hushed up by the other hands.

"It's the truth, I tell you," Rawhide Robinson said. "And that ain't even the strangest thing. I noticed my bedroll was soaked plumb through as well. So I kept on a-pourin' water out of that boot and called a couple of them other cowboys to come over and help. They tore apart my bedroll and starting wringin' out them sougans, and I kept up tryin' to empty out my boots, and they kept twistin' water out of my bedclothes, and so on. You never seen so much water; soon enough we was up to our knees in the stuff, and no end of it in sight.

"Every man among us was lappin' it up like a pack of parched possum hounds. And them cattle wasted no time tanking up on it, either, nor the saddle stock. We filled up the water barrels on the chuckwagon and the hoodlum wagon, and filled every pot, pan, kettle, cup, and can we could lay hands on.

"I'll tell you boys, that dream was a godsend. Had it not been for that water, we'd have all perished out in that desert, man and animal alike. As it was, we was able to push on, and we followed that herd out of that desert and on to our destination."

"%^+\#*!" McCarty said.

"I gotta tell you, Rawhide, even I ain't believin' that tale."

"Well why not, Enos? It's the truth just as I've told it."

"No way. I've smelled them rancid feet of yours many a night around this campfire. And there ain't no way anyone could survive drinking water that came out of your boots."

CHAPTER EIGHT

In which Rawhide Robinson saves a damsel in distress

The night was calm and the cattle were quiet as Rawhide Robinson took his turn at night guard, riding around and around the herd, eyes and ears alert for any trouble. But, this night, there was none.

I was a child and she was a child,

In this kingdom by the sea, Rawhide Robinson said, reciting a poem by Edgar Allan Poe.

But we loved with a love that was more than love—

I and my Annabel Lee, Doak heard as they crossed on one of their big circles around the lazing cattle.

When next they approached and passed and parted, Doak listened to a snippet of song:

> *We loved each other then, Lorena*
> *More than we ever dared to tell*
> *And what might have been, Lorena*
> *Had but our loving prospered well*
> *But then, 'tis past, the years have gone*
> *I'll not call up their shadowy forms*
> *I'll say to them, "Lost years, sleep on*
> *Sleep on, nor heed life's pelting storms. . . .*

Next trip, it was back to poetry as the cowboys drew near in the night. Doak reined up to roll a smoke, then stopped his saddle pal in mid-stanza.

But thy eternal summer shall not fade,
Nor lose possession of that fair thou owest,
Nor shall death brag thou wandrest in his shade,
When in eternal lines to time thou growest,—

Doak said, "What's that you're saying, Rawhide?"

"It's called Sonnet 18."

"Where's that come from?"

"Why, that particular verse was penned by one William Shakespeare, the Bard of Avon."

"Think I've heard that before," Doak said. "How's it start?"

Shall I compare thee to a summer's day?

Thou art more lovely and more temperate. . . . Rawhide recited.

Doak said, "Thought so. Knew I'd heard it. Well, we'd best ride."

And so they did, circling the herd until their shift ended and Arizona and another hand rode out, yawning faces smeared with sleep, to relieve them. A few hours' rest soon passed and the crew spent another ordinary day on the trail, moving the cattle onward toward Kansas.

"Rawhide, I got a question for you," Doak said around the rim of his coffee cup as the cowboys settled in for another ordinary evening around the campfire.

"Sure," said Rawhide. "Ask away."

"Them songs you sing on night guard, and them poems you say. Seems like they're all about women. And mostly all sad stories—you're always singing 'Annie Laurie' and 'Lorena,' and sayin' that 'Highwayman' poem or 'Annabel Lee' or one of them Shakespeare love poems."

Rawhide Robinson waited, unsure if there was question in there or not.

"Well?" said Doak.

"Well what?" said Rawhide Robinson.

"Why is that?"

"Well, son, lots of poems and songs are about men loving women. Most all of them, I reckon."

"Sure, but not all of them's sad and dismal like those ones."

Rawhide Robinson waited.

"So," Doak said, "I was just wonderin'. . . ."

"Yes?"

"Some girl somewhere, sometime, break your heart?"

Rawhide said nothing; just sat on his bedroll, propped against his saddle in his ordinary way, studying the coffee in his tin cup as he rotated it around and around with the fingers of both hands.

"C'mon, @&^)+!" McCarty said. "You're all the time a-talkin' but you don't never tell no stories about you and women. What's the deal?"

"Well, boys, it's kind of hard to talk about," Rawhide Robinson said. "But Doak has got it about right. I was in love once, some years back. And all I ended up with out of that deal was a lot of sad memories and a heart busted into a thousand little pieces. . . ."

"Oh, that, and a high-bred black stallion of fine European stock."

A strained silence broke when Enos said, "So, Rawhide, you gonna tell us about it?"

"Well?" said Doak.

"I'll tell it," Rawhide Robinson said. "But I'm warning you, it's a long story."

"*#@&+=!" McCarty said.

"Hush up," Arizona said.

"Tell us," Enos said.

"Here's what happened," Rawhide said to start the story. "One time after following a herd to the railhead in Kansas, I thought to follow them cattle the rest of the way—just out of curiosity, you know, to see what there was to see. So I took me a job on the cattle cars and rode all the way to Chicago.

"Boys, you ain't never seen such a place. You could get a crick in your neck just walkin' around them streets gawkin' up at all those tall buildings. More people in a city block than they got in any whole town I'd ever been in before.

"Noise. Land sakes, you never heard such a racket. And it don't never get quiet, even in the middle of the night. And a feller's nose gets plumb overworked trying to sort out all the smells. Garbage. Smoke. Rotten vegetables. All manner of cooking. Manure. Sweat. Sewer. Spoiled meat. Wet dogs. Just thinking about it brings that stink back to my nose.

"Anyway, there I was in Chicago, Illinois, just wanderin' the streets takin' in the sights when I heard all this screamin' and carryin' on and crashin' and bangin' and I turns around for a look-see and there's this bright red carriage with a fancy lady aboard bouncing down the street behind a runaway team of fine-looking bay horses—about sixteen hands high, they was, white stockings on all four legs and a little diamond on each of their foreheads, fancy red ribbons braided into their manes, tails knotted up all nice—"

"C'mon, Robinson! Get on with the +/%*#@ story. Nobody cares what the horses looked like!"

"Pipe down, McCarty."

"Talk on, Rawhide."

"Them horses, they was plumb panicked I tell you. Wall-eyed, ears pinned back, poundin' down that crowded street for all they was worth. That carriage is a-whippin' and a-wobblin' and a-swayin', up on one set of wheels then the other. Folks was screamin' and runnin' and diving every which way to get clear. A garbage wagon overturned when the nag pullin' it bolted. That carriage bounced over a curbstone and knocked over a vegetable cart—I'm tellin' you boys, it was a wreck already, and looking for all it was worth for a way to get worse.

"Well, in the middle of it all, lookin' on wide-eyed with jaw a-danglin', was a police officer aboard a big ol' sorrel gelding. Big horse, seventeen hands if he was an inch, heavy in the neck and shoulders—"

"*%>@$! Enough with the horses!"

"All right, all right—don't get your whiskers in a twist, Mc-Carty. Anyway, I pulled that policeman off that horse and swung aboard and lit out down the street after that runaway carriage. Managed to pull even with that team and bailed out of the saddle and onto the back of the off-side horse. It took some doing, but I hauled on the bits and twisted them horses' necks enough to convince them to give up the chase.

"When finally I got them calmed down enough that I didn't figure they'd stampede again, I thought to check on the passenger."

Rawhide Robinson paused in the telling and ambled over to the fire to warm up the coffee in his cup. The cowboys fussed and fidgeted, awaiting the resumption of the story. Finally, when he figured he'd tortured his audience enough, Rawhide Robinson continued.

"I'll tell you boys, my heart was a-gallopin' like them runaway horses, but when I laid eyes on that girl it plumb stopped. Her hat had blown off in all the commotion and her hair come undone, so she had all these dangling tresses of hair the color of them blood-bay horses and shining in the sun like a silver concho. Eyes green as leaves on a mesquite tree and lips red as the cherry on an ice cream sundae. Her skin was white as a hen's egg, all except for her cheeks, which was blushed the shade of a rose in winter and sprinkled with freckles like wildflowers across a mountain meadow.

"When finally my breath came back and my heart started up again, I yanked off my hat and asked was she okay and she set in to jabberin' in some lingo I never heard before. Soon enough this fellow in a fancy uniform runs up. Turns out he was her driver and had just stepped down to purchase a hot chocolate from a street vendor for the lady when whatever it was went and upset them horses. He kept up pourin' thanks over me like sorghum over cornbread till I could hush him up. But, he said, had that girl been hurt, her father and brothers'd have shot him for dereliction of duty.

"Anyways, they bantered back and forth for a while and he said she wanted me to come to supper that evening at their hotel so her family could thank me proper for savin' her bacon. I said there wasn't no need, but that driver got the address for my rooming house and allowed as he would be around later to gather me up.

"Well, boys, it turns out that girl was a princess."

"<=&}%#*!"

"It's the honest truth, McCarty. She was a member of the royal family of Eurostandovialand, and the whole tribe of them was on a Grand Adventure Tour and Hunting Expedition of North America. When I got there, to where they was stayin', I mean, they was all set up for a fancy banquet in a big ballroom at that hotel.

"But, it turns out, it weren't no banquet at all—that was how them royals took all their meals. There was a few of them seated around the end of a banquet table that took up the whole middle of the room, with a bunch of other folks—all their staff and servants and such, as it turned out—at rows of little round tables all around the rest of the room.

"Sittin' at the head of the table was that girl's father, who was King of Eurostandovialand, and I'll tell you the headgear that fellow was wearing made my thirteen-gallon Stetson hat plumb inconspicuous.

"Why, he had on what looked like an upside-down chamber pot, only it was made of gold and white fur and red velvet and black leather—turns out red was the royal color of Eurostan-dovialand, so they had lots of stuff that particular crimson shade. Anyway, his hat had shiny jewels and baubles around the headband and a gold spike thing poking up on top.

"Other than that and a cape, he was dressed pretty much like a banker and so was the rest of the men crowded around one end of that long table. And that girl, my goodness, she looked even prettier than she had before.

"Some feller in a fancy uniform walked me over to the table and introduced me to King Trifle and all the rest of them. There was three men besides the King, who turned out to be his sons: Prince Shadrach, Prince Meshach, and Prince Abednego. And there was Princess Crystalline, whose acquaintance, of course, I had already made.

"The King, he spoke proper English and so did them princes to one degree or another. Princess Crystalline, she savvied the American lingo somewhat, but all that had left her in that escapade with the carriage, which was why she was blathering so at the time.

"After a hearty round of thanks and a bunch of toasts with wine in crystal glasses, we set in to eatin'. I'll tell you boys, that meal went on for hours with them folks in uniform takin' away China plates fast as you could empty them, and replacing them with another, every one covered with some other tasty treat. I swear, I didn't even know what it was I was eatin' half the time, but I never had such tasty vittles.

"Finally, Princess Crystalline excused herself and the men-folk settled back for some serious scratchin' and belchin', accompanied by brandy and cigars. The King informed me that come spring, his expedition would head west for some buffalo hunting in Dakota Territory, then make their way to California and winter over there before sailing for the Orient then back to Eurostandovialand when they got around to it. When they found out I'd spent some time in Dakota and knew that country, they engaged me as a guide. For a right handsome salary, I might add.

"$*(?@#*! You ain't never been to no Dakota Territory!" McCarty said.

"Nonsense, boy. I spent a winter working on a ranch there. Cold! You ain't never seen such cold! Why, one time—"

"Rawhide!" Enos said. "Don't be changin' horses in the middle of a stream. Get back to your story!"

"Well, all right then. But remind me sometime to tell you about that winter in Dakota Territory. Now, where was I?"

"That King of Eurostanhoovia or whatever it is hired you on as a guide," Arizona said.

"Right. So, anyway, they convinced me to hang around Chicago for the winter and they'd pay me a passel of cash to help care for the stock and arrange for such provisions as they'd need. Then I was to act as scout and guide once we set out for the Western plains come the spring grass.

"I took them up on the offer, of course, as I was plumb smitten with Princess Crystalline. We spent hours and days together, me and that girl. We drove all around town in that fancy red carriage, strolled through the city parks in the evening, went to shows and the opry from time to time, sampled the fare at a bunch of eatin' houses, and come to enjoy one another's company a right smart.

"Most times King Trifle sent a chaperone along, and her big brothers, Princes Shadrach, Meshach, and Abednego, threatened that if I so much as laid a finger on her they'd break it off at the bottom knuckle and feed it to me. But, we did manage to slip away now and again for some serious cuddlin' and kissin'.

"Come the spring thaw and the greening of the grass we lined out the wagons and headed west," Rawhide Robinson said as he tossed the dregs of his coffee, slid full length onto his bedroll, and plopped his Stetson over his face.

"But that's a story for another day."

He withstood the entreaties of his saddle pals to continue the tale, reminding them of the need for sleep ahead of another long day on the trail.

"I ain't as young as I once was," Rawhide Robinson reminded them. "But don't you boys fret none. I'll tell the rest of it another time."

"&^>*@#!"

"Hush up and go to sleep, McCarty," someone said.

CHAPTER NINE

In which Rawhide Robinson falls in love

"Well, boys, we lit out from Chicago and headed west," Rawhide Robinson said in introducing the continuation of his tale after another ordinary day trailing cattle. The crew had bolted their beans and biscuits and topped off their tin cups with scalding coffee and settled in for an early evening around the campfire, eager for another round of being regaled by the raconteur Rawhide Robinson.

A few of the hands had awl and whang leather at hand, busying themselves with repairs to headstalls, saddles, boots, chaps, and such as they listened. But most were empty handed and empty headed, so as not to miss a single word of the tale. Even McCarty's eyes gleamed with anticipation.

"And we headed west in style. A man could use up a good chunk of daylight just ridin' from one end of that Eurostandovialand Royal Family Grand Adventure Tour and Hunting Expedition of North America wagon train to the other. There was supply wagons, baggage wagons, chuckwagons, tent wagons, armory wagons, spring wagons, and a passel of fancy crimson red carriages like that one in that runaway I told you about, all strung out for miles.

"Looked like a wagon train of sodbusters headed for Oregon, except no collection of settlers was ever so well outfitted as them Eurostandovialanders. Can't even say how many folks was on that expedition, but it was a passel of 'em. All that, just so's a king, three princes, and a princess could do a little huntin'," Rawhide Robinson said.

"And hunt we did. The country thereabouts was woods giving way to prairie, with plenty of it cleared for farming. So, there was deer thereabouts, bears, elk now and then; why, we even bagged a moose one day. There was wolverines and badgers, wolves and squirrels. Birds, of course. Ducks of more kinds than I ever saw, and geese.

"Them royals'd shoot at anything. And, the fact is, boys, they'd hit most everything they shot at. Every one of 'em a crack shot; made no never mind if it was a rifle, shotgun, fowling piece, or pistol, they could all shoot.

"Why, for several days there we got in amongst them passenger pigeons they got back east, and you never seen such shooting. That King Trifle and them Princes Shadrach, Meshach, and Abednego shot them birds on the wing, shot 'em on the ground, shot 'em out of trees—didn't much matter, they'd shoot 'em by the wagonload all day long, day after day."

"#&*@4=!" said McCarty. "There ain't that many birds nowhere, nohow."

"I'm a-telling you the honest truth. And not only was them passenger pigeons as thick as the skeeters on Buffalo Bayou, they was as dumb as sheep," Rawhide Robinson said. "Why, one day them princes soaked a sack of wheat in corn liquor and spread it out on the ground for them birds to eat. Pretty soon there was drunken passenger pigeons staggerin' all over the place, fallin' down when they tried to walk and bouncin' off trees when they tried to fly. That day, them boys didn't even bother to shoot—they'd just gather them birds up by handfuls and wring their necks.

"But they soon tired of that, and the birds was thinnin' out considerable. I suppose them dumb pigeons finally realized it wasn't safe in that neighborhood. So them boys would take a live one and tether him to a string staked to the ground. That pigeon would flap and flop around there trying to fly away, which would rouse the curiosity of whatever other pigeons was in the area and they'd flock around in droves to see what was goin' on. Which, of course, was what them princes intended—but was not too healthy for them birds.

"Thank goodness King Trifle got tired of shooting them birds after baggin' a pile of 'em as high as that there Pikes Peak I told you about one time. But, once he realized there weren't no more sport in it, he ordered the Expedition to move on.

"Like I said, I was mighty glad of that for by then I'd had my fill of them pigeons. We ate 'em roasted and fried, boiled and baked. We had 'em in soups and stews, pies and pastries. We ate 'em for breakfast, we ate 'em for dinner, we ate 'em for supper. Even that whole crew of fancy cooks was runnin' out of ways to cook them birds. I've never been happier than the day we run dry of passenger pigeons. I swear I was startin' to sprout feathers."

All the talk about food started Rawhide Robinson's stomach to rumbling, so he sauntered over to the chuckwagon and cadged a cold biscuit from the bread bin and refilled his coffee cup before nesting back into his bedroll and resuming his tale.

"Once we got out onto the prairies a ways, we started comin' onto buffalo herds. I'd ride out on a big circle and locate a bunch, then hightail it back to camp and lead the king and them princes out for some shooting. They'd make a stand sometimes; sometimes they'd set out on a chase and hunt from horseback. They even took up bows and arrows and tried shootin' buffalo Indian style.

"I tell you, boys, we shipped a goodly number of hides back to Chicago. Had wagons makin' down-and-back trips all the time, heaped with buffalo hides on the way to town and loaded with grub and supplies and a good deal of powder on the way back.

"Sometimes I'd join the boys on the hunt, sometimes I'd just spectate and lend the servants a hand with the skinning. But we didn't have to skin too many for too long. Fact is, after a while we didn't even have to shoot no more buffalo to get hides," Rawhide Robinson said around a mouthful of coffee.

"How's that?" Enos wondered.

"Well, soon enough them buffalo come to realize—just as them passenger pigeons had—that them Eurostandovialand royals was such handy shots that it just weren't no use to resist. So the buffalo just took to wandering right up close to camp and sheddin' their skins, then driftin' back onto the prairie till they growed a new hide."

"&?<%=@#!"

"Why, McCarty, that's just how it happened. Precisely so as I said. I wouldn't lie to you."

"}*&*#! Robinson, there just ain't no way of that happening."

"What, you mean a buffalo losin' its hide?"

"No such thing," McCarty said.

"Don't be daft, boy. Why, just looky yonder—there's a buffalo hide right there under Enos's bedroll and there sure ain't no buffalo wearin' it."

"+@#&^*!" McCarty said.

"Pipe down, McCarty," Doak said.

"He got you again, kid," Arizona said.

"*<$*=*#!" McCarty said.

"So what happened next?" another cowboy said.

"Well, we just wandered along thataway all summer long, not never in no hurry. See, that Eurostandovialand Royal Family Grand Adventure Tour and Hunting Expedition of North America wasn't in any hurry to get anywhere. So we'd just ease along until we found some good huntin' or interesting scenery and we'd make camp—set up a town, more like—and idle around thereabouts until the king or them princes got bored.

"Which suited me just fine, you see, for all that lazy time in camp gave me plenty of opportunities to spark Princess Crystalline. We spent hours just sittin' and talkin', which helped her English considerable. She got to where she could converse in fine style. But I never did catch on to that gobbledygook they speak in Eurostandovialand. Never made no sense to me nohow. Always sounded to me like they was trying to wrap their tongues around a mouthful of marbles, or maybe clear their throats or palaver through their proboscis."

"What!? #$(*@+, Robinson, you're at it again. What's that fifty-cent word you're tossin' around?"

"Proboscis? Why, that's another name for that appendage hangin' off the front of your physiognomy."

"*>+#$@!"

"Why McCarty, the meaning is as plain as the nose on your face," Rawhide said.

"&%#@(!"

Doak said, "Your nose, McCarty. It's your nose. Now hush. Now get on with it, Rawhide."

"Where was I? All right, I remember. So, anyway, me and the princess sat and we talked and we walked and we rode and we took buggy rides and we even contrived to steal a kiss every now and then. But the king, he kept a pretty close eye on us—leastways he had some of his people watch that we didn't get up to no good.

"And Shadrach, Meshach, and Abednego kept on remindin' me in no uncertain terms that them guns of theirs could ventilate all kinds of varmints, be they the four- or two-legged variety. Including me, if I was to get crosswise of their baby sister. Who wasn't no baby, by the way.

"Still and all, all that discouragement didn't keep me from getting all aflutter and foolish over that girl, nor did it keep her from fallin' plumb in love with me."

"&(&?<#*!" McCarty said. "What would any purty girl want to do with the likes of you? And never mind a princess! You're plumb common. And old and ugly to boot."

"Mind your manners, button. I cut quite the dashing figure in them days, if I do say so myself."

"You'd have to say so, 'cause sure as shootin' nobody else would say it."

Said Enos, "Hush up, McCarty. Me and Rawhide wasn't always as old and used up as we seem to be to a youngster such as yourself. But, truth is, you ain't never goin' to be as young as you are now, yourself. You just wait and see. Meantime, hush. Talk on, Rawhide."

"Yeah," Doak said. "What happened with you and that gal?"

"Well, since she ain't here beside me you can imagine it didn't end well. But just now I'm in need of some shuteye. I got my shift on night guard to ride in a couple hours and we got a river to cross tomorrow. So you all will just have to leave me happy in love, at least for the time being."

And, with that, Rawhide Robinson hunkered down in his sougans, plopped his thirteen-gallon Texas hat over his eyes, and readied himself for some satisfying snoring.

CHAPTER TEN

In which Rawhide Robinson loses his one true love but gains one fine horse

"Arizona! Watch that brindle steer!" Enos hollered.

The cowboy called Arizona reined his horse downstream to encourage the animal to rejoin the herd. The steer had decided to quit the bunch midstream, in the only part of the river where the bottom got too deep for footwork and swimming was required.

As Arizona and his waterlogged pony worked through the current, the cowboy saw heading off the steer was a lost cause, so unslung his catch rope and snaked a loop toward the animal and managed to pull the slack tight around its horns before the twine floated away. Taking his hard dallies around the saddle horn, Arizona reined back toward the bank with the unruly bovine in tow.

Seeing the lone steer downstream, supposedly swimming for freedom, a half dozen other cow critters, then more, peeled off the herd and headed that direction, only to be impeded in their progress by Arizona's stretched lariat. The churning steers plowed and piled into one another as they struck the barrier, their mass and momentum dragging Arizona, his horse, and the tethered steer into the melee. The horse pivoted, wrapping the rope around Arizona's back. Try as he might, the cowboy could not slip his dallies, the wet rope being stretched taut and in a bind. The cow pony fought gamely, pawing at the water but found no traction.

The young cowboy McCarty, seeing the rider's misfortune, urged his horse forward, finally reaching the churning knot of steers struggling against the rope barrier that stretched nearly full circle around them. McCarty pawed at a vest pocket, finally grasping a jackknife, and he pulled the blade free with his teeth.

He slashed at the taut twine, parting the soaked rope. Slowly, the tangled mess of hides and horns drifted apart and each panicked animal floated free, swimming toward either bank. McCarty and Arizona managed to get them headed and all pointed in the proper direction, pushing them up the opposite bank and back toward the herd, then rode back into the river and their jobs as if nothing untoward had happened.

Later, as the crew gathered around the campfire to enjoy an ordinary supper of biscuits and beans, Arizona offered McCarty his thanks.

"%&*@=," McCarty said. "It weren't nothing."

"Nothin' my eye," Arizona said. "You saved my bacon sure as shootin'. I'm beholdin' to you."

"No different than when Robinson fished me out of the river a while back," McCarty said. "Ain't no big deal."

Enos corrected the young cowboy. "Like it or no, that was some heroics on your part. Same as when Rawhide saved your hide. Anytime someone saves a life it's a big deal. You keep on bein' in the right place at the right time, McCarty, and you'll make a hand yet. Lordy, boy, you might even end up in one of Rawhide's stories."

"/>&#*+!"

The tired cowboys topped off tin cups of coffee and settled in for the evening's festivities. Doak opened the ball.

"Say, Rawhide, how about finishin' up that story about your hunting trip with all that royalty, and your romance with that Princess from Eurostandalia."

"It's Eurostandovialand," Rawhide Robinson said as he nestled into his bedroll and propped himself against his saddle.

"Aahh, the fair Princess Crystalline," he reminisced, once settled. "I'm telling you boys, that girl was prettier than a speckled pup. And when we chanced to steal a kiss, her lips was sweeter than hollow-tree honey, and them kisses more intoxicating than Kentucky whiskey. Fine times, they was, that I spent with that girl.

"But, back to the story. As I was saying, we wandered across the high plains wherever adventure beckoned and wherever King Trifle took a notion. And boys, we did see some sights. You all ever hear of Yellowstone Park? Well, we went there on one of our little outings and I'm here to tell you it's a strange place. Things there ain't like they are anywhere else I ever been or even heard tell of."

"How do you mean?" Enos asked, eventually breaking another of Rawhide Robinson's stretched-out silences.

"Well, for one thing, that place is all afire underground. You can be riding through otherwise ordinary-lookin' piney woods and all around there'll be little wisps of smoke and steam leaking out of the ground. And, here and there, there's little ponds full of steamy water, some so hot it's boiling. Sometimes, things just plumb explode. The ground starts shaking and rumbling and pretty soon scalding hot water's shootin' up out of the ground high as the trees."

"I've heard of such things," Enos said. "But I never imagined it to be true."

"Oh, it's true, all right. They call them spouts geysers, and there's a bunch of them. Some places they're thick as ticks on a redbone hound—water spurting up everywhere and all over the place. Why, there's one big one they called Old Faithful, on account of it shoots off every hour or thereabouts, just like clockwork. Which proved to be right handy to our party."

Again, Rawhide Robinson paused for effect.

"@#<*$!" McCarty exploded like a Yellowstone geyser. "Get on with it!"

"Well, you see, what that Old Faithful geyser amounted to was a vacation of sorts for the washerwomen on that trip. Rather than heatin' up tubs of water and scrubbin' duds on washboards in the usual way, why they'd just toss all the wash down the hole of that geyser. Then, an hour later, or however long they figured them clothes needed soaking, Old Faithful would cough it all back up, all clean and tidy. 'Course they still had to hang it out to dry, but even then they'd just string a clothesline over a crack in the ground and all that hot air coming up would dry it out in no time.

"Cooks had it pretty easy, too. See, the folks that run that Yellowstone place plant little garden plots here and there so's they don't have to freight in so much grub. Come mealtime, them kitchen helpers of the King's would just dig up some root crops—turnips, beets, carrots, onions, spuds, and such. And, sure as I'm born, they was already all cooked up tender and tasty by that hot ground. Didn't even need salt.

"From time to time, them chefs'd dump a barrel of beans and toss a side of bacon into one of them hot ponds and it'd cook up all on its own. Didn't even need stirring, on account of them bubbling pots'd do that for you, too. And fish! Land sakes, you never saw so many fat trout. Big long ones," Rawhide Robinson said, stretching his arms full length.

"+=$*/#!" McCarty said. "I suppose they was already cooked too."

"No, of course they wasn't! Don't be silly. But here's what we did. We'd get a bunch of us lined up across a stream or in the shallows of a lake, and we'd just move along slow-like and drive them fish—just like you would a herd of cows—to a place where some of that hot water from them ponds or geysers dumped in, and just hold them there until they was cooked to a turn. Took a little work, but it was worth it. Never tasted such fish. I swear, boys, them trout never even had bones."

"@#$%^&!"

Said Doak, "Hush up, McCarty. Rawhide, that's enough jawin' about food. What about that there princess?"

"I do believe you're smitten, Doak," Enos said.

"I reckon that's so. Been so long since I laid eyes on a woman that just hearin' about one is pure pleasure. C'mon, Rawhide. Get on with it."

"It's a sad story, I'm afraid," Rawhide Robinson said. "Least-ways the end of it is. But while it lasted, being with Princess Crystalline was as pleasant as strollin' past the pearly gates for a visit to heaven.

"It all came to an end on the high desert out in the Oregon country. Them princes Shadrach, Meshach, and Abednego caught me and Princess Crystalline cuddlin' in the shade of one of the chuckwagons one evening under a full moon. Upset those boys a right smart, it did, and they marched the two of us off to King Trifle's tent. Them princes informed the King we'd been caught with arms entwined and lips-a-smackin' and he set in to questioning us.

"Princess Crystalline informed her old daddy that we were plumb in love and there just weren't no help for it. I allowed as that were true, and stated my intentions to make that girl my wife.

"That set King Trifle off, as you might imagine. He lectured us long and loud about royal bloodlines and purity of the nobil-ity and diplomatic relations with other dominions and a passel of other high-minded blather that didn't make no sense to me whatsoever.

"What it come down to in the end was that I weren't nothin' but a commoner, a plumb common commoner at that, and an

American besides, and in nowise a fit companion for his imperial daughter. He allowed as I was a fine guide and a crack-shot hunter and a good hand with a horse, but no more than a servant—and that servants don't cut no mustard in Eurostandovialand. So, he told me, if I intended to keep my head attached to the rest of me I had better not get within sniffin' distance of Princess Crystalline ever again.

" 'Course that King had took a liking to me, and he felt bad about it and all, but that was just the way it was. He allowed as they was breakin' camp in the morning and headin' south towards California, and that I was to choose another direction of travel and leave right that minute for parts unknown—so long as they wasn't California.

"By way of apology and in payment for services rendered, as he put it, he had my kack cinched to the back of a big black stallion name of Othello. I'd admired that horse for a good long time, as he was as fine an example of horseflesh as Princess Crystalline was of womanhood—not that I'd of traded, you understand, but sad as I was to lose that girl I was plumb pleased to get that horse.

"Now Othello, he was the result of careful selective cross-breeding of the finest Eurostandovialand stock, as the King told it. Like as I said, he was black. Dark as the inside of a cow's belly on a dark night, he was, but he gleamed bright as sunshine. Big, that horse was, and strong as a draft animal, but fine-boned and fancy-formed like a racehorse. It was a plumb pleasure to ride away from them royals aboard Othello, even if I was leavin' my poor broken heart behind in the possession of the divine Princess Crystalline.

"All three of them Princes—Shadrach, Meshach, and Abed-nego—escorted me a good ways out of camp and advised me to 'ride west until my hat floats.'

"So I did."

CHAPTER ELEVEN

In which Rawhide Robinson crosses the sea, horseback

Memories of Princess Crystalline dampened Rawhide Robinson's spirits and he spent the remainder of the evening brooding on his bedroll. His saddle pals sensed his sadness and allowed him the silence of his sorrow. But, as on any other ordinary evening on the trail, he had his shift on night guard to attend to. Again, Doak shared the assignment, and as they rode he heard snatches of yet another sad poem, drifting like a blue, wispy mist in Rawhide Robinson's wake:

> *Lasca used to ride*
> *On a mouse-grey mustang close to my side,*
> *With blue serape and bright-belled spur;*
> *I laughed with joy as I looked at her!*

And, later:

> *She would hunger that I might eat,*
> *Would take the bitter and leave me the sweet;*

Later, still:

> *As over us surged the sea of steers,*
> *Blows that beat blood into my eyes,*
> *And when I could rise—*
> *Lasca was dead!*

And again:

> *And the buzzard sails on,*
> *And comes and is gone,*
> *Stately as a ship at sea.*
> *And I wonder why I do not care*
> *For the things that are, like the things that were.*
> *Does half my heart lie buried there*
> *In Texas, down by the Rio Grande.*

But Rawhide Robinson's constitution was naturally averse to misery, so a night's sleep and a day's work rejuvenated his mood.

"Sorry, boys, about my little bout of ennui last evening," he said as the crew wrapped up another ordinary supper of bacon, biscuits, and beans.

"Of what?" McCarty asked.

"Ennui."

"What's that mean?"

"You know, ennui—languor, lassitude, listlessness."

"@+[#&*! Robinson, whyn't you leave off with them fifty-cent words and say what you mean!"

"Gloom, McCarty," Rawhide said. "A sort of bored sadness. The blues."

"Then say so! If you're sad, say you're sad."

"English is a rich language, my friend. We got plenty of words, to my way of thinking, and we might just as well use them."

"?/%{=#! If you feel bad, you feel bad. That's all there is to it."

Rawhide Robinson mulled that one over for a moment, then held forth.

"But what of depressed? Despondent? Disheartened? Demoralized? Discouraged? Dejected? Despair? Downhearted? Downcast? Disconsolate? Dispirited? Deflated? Discontent? And that's just the words that start with 'D' that come to mind."

"Ain't nobody needs that many words," McCarty said. "Ain't no sense clutterin' up your head with all that nonsense."

Arizona said, "Wouldn't hurt you none to improve your vocabulary some, McCarty. Maybe replace some of that profanity with some other words. I suspect there's plenty of room in that head of yours for some new words."

">+@4&#!" McCarty said. "There ain't even that many words in most books. Maybe that's it, Robinson—you've spent too much of your time reading. That's probably where you came up with all them &*@#& stories of yours, too. Out of books."

Rawhide Robinson smiled. "I confess to more than my share of reading, all right. But I'm here to tell you that the stories I tell you didn't come out of no book. Every word of every one is as true as the sunrise, drawn from a life rich with experience and adventure."

"*%@#+!"

"Speakin' of true stories," Arizona chimed in, "How's about that one about crossin' the ocean you was goin' to tell us?"

"Tell it, Rawhide. C'mon," Doak said. "Don't pay McCarty no never mind."

"Oh, McCarty will be all right," Rawhide said. "It's just that he ain't quite dry behind the ears. Or quite filled out between 'em."

"*(?#%!"

"Put a lid on it, McCarty," a cowboy said. "Tell us the story, Rawhide."

Always accommodating, Rawhide Robinson did just that.

He told of his solitary journey across the rugged Cascade Mountains, never stopping for food or drink, having lost his appetite when he lost the fair Crystalline. Of riding through the verdant Willamette Valley, stopping to rest only when Othello wearied and refused to go on, then wrapping himself in a saddle blanket and huddling under a tree until awakening to find his horse refreshed and cropping grass nearby, then saddling up and riding on, ever westward. Of climbing up one side of the Coast Range and down the other, oblivious to the welts and wounds of whipping tree limbs; not even noticing the perpetual wet that permeated his clothing, turning outerwear into a soggy shell and underclothing into a sodden skin.

And he told of his eventual arrival at the Pacific shore.

He told how, seated aboard Othello, he gazed, amazed, at the waves pounding the rocks, realizing for the first time in a long time that he was alive, and a resident of a magnificent world— and, yet, a world in which he had little interest.

He said how he and Othello watched the foam skitter up and down the narrow beach. Saw seabirds wheeling overhead, sharp wings slicing through the damp air, and sharp cries cutting through the sound of the pounding surf. And how he looked westward, ever westward, recalling the advice of Princes Shadrach, Meshach, and Abednego to "keep riding west until your hat floats."

Steeling himself, Rawhide Robinson rode into the surf.

"I hardly knew what to expect," he said. "Other than crossing rivers on cattle drives, the deepest water I'd ever been in was in a bathtub. Never did learn to swim."

"&*@#+?^<!" McCarty said. "You rode out into that ocean not knowing how to swim? That's plumb crazy, even for one of your stories."

"At the time, I might well have been. Plumb crazy, I mean. Guess I didn't really care if I lived or died. Figured that horse would just swim out into that water until he was spent, and we'd sink to the bottom of the deep blue sea and that would be the end of us.

"Thing was, that Othello just kept swimming and swimming and swimming. That thirteen-gallon hat of mine never got so much as damp, let alone wanting to float. I don't know how many days and nights that horse kept paddling ever westward—but it was a good, long time for certain. After a while, I sort of got over the worst of my sadness and started in to liking that little ride across the water.

"Why, there was fishes of all shapes and sizes. More than you can imagine. Long skinny ones and short fat ones. There was fishes that looked like snakes. Fishes that would swim standing up and had heads that made them look like little horses. I saw fishes almost as round as a dinner plate and just as flat.

"Some of them ocean critters had eyes on little stems, others had both eyes on one side of their heads. I saw some that looked like they were flying through the water, and there were even fishes that could jump out of the water and fly through the air."

"&★@#)=!"

"It's the honest truth, son. And that ain't the half of it. There were fishes in every color you've ever seen and plenty of colors you never even imagined. They had stripes and spots and speckles and splotches. Some of them even glowed in the dark.

"Anyway, along about that time, Othello started to flag a little. I could feel in my knees he was tiring. Lucky for us, along about then this herd of dolphins started swimming along with us. They'd buck and play in them waves as we'd swim along, looking like they were having a real good time. Why, I swear them dolphins was even smiling. From time to time I'd just slide off old Othello and sit astraddle one of them dolphin fish so that my horse could rest awhile.

"That helped some, but he was still giving out a little more each day. I'll tell you, I was riding pretty low in the water for a time, there. Then here comes this big old whale a-swimming by, and Othello climbed right up on his back and just stood there, riding along with the sea breeze a-riffling his mane—once it got dried out, that is. Got all the rest he needed, that way."

"★(>$@&#★! You meaning us to believe that you and that

horse of yours rode a whale?"

"We sure enough did, McCarty, whether you believe it or don't."

"And I suppose that there =?#^&* whale carried you on across that ocean to dry land."

"No, he didn't. And he didn't swallow us up and spit us out, like old Jonah in the Good Book, neither."

Enos asked, "So what happened, Rawhide?"

Rawhide Robinson rambled over to the coffeepot for a refill before continuing. The cowboys fussed and fidgeted as they waited, breathing a collective sigh of relief when he once again nestled down into his bedroll.

"Once Othello got rested up, I climbed aboard again and we lit out across the water again, having a good old time. Then this sailing ship happened by, and them sailors, thinking us in trouble, fished us out of that ocean with a big net and took us aboard their ship. They were on the way to the Sandwich Islands, and not having anything else to do at the time, I decided to go along for the ride.

"It was a mighty long trip, on top of what Othello and I had already traveled. But, now, on that ship, we at least had regular food. They fed me with the crew, and most of what they fed us was rancid pork out of leaky hogsheads and salted fish. Never ate so much fish in my life. Fact is, other than trout now and again, about the onliest thing I ever ate that came out of the water was beef from a steer that had once stood in a mud puddle.

"We finally made it to those Sandwich Islands," Rawhide Robinson said, "which was a good thing. You see, them islands were overrun with cow critters and what that place needed more than anything was a cowboy.

"That cowboy being me.

"Which story I will relate on another occasion, around

another campfire."

"Aw, c'mon!"

"Tell us, Rawhide!"

"Don't quit now!"

"*&#@<$&!"

But Rawhide Robinson plopped his thirteen-gallon hat over his face, closed his eyes, and dreamed the dreams of the innocent until awakened for his duty riding night guard.

Chapter Twelve

In which Rawhide Robinson saves the Hawaiians from cantankerous cattle

Nothing out of the ordinary occurred on the drive the next day; the crew moved the cattle without incident. Even the bunch quitters were, by now, resigned to the routine of staying with the herd, moseying northward in the mind-numbing humdrum of the trail to the rails. No river to cross. No wolves worrying the herd. No lurking cattle thieves. No storms brewing.

And so the drovers were eager for the mild change in routine an evening around the campfire might offer. Rawhide Robinson's arrival ashore on the Sandwich Islands promised adventure, and they were impatient to experience it, if only vicariously.

"You've heard tell of paradise," Rawhide Robinson surmised as he started the tale. "Well, I'll tell you, the Sandwich Islands is about as close to that kind of place as you'll likely find. On this earth, leastways. Never gets cold, not too hot. Sunshine most all the time, other than maybe a cooling rain in the afternoon. Sandy beaches and a beautiful blue-green sea.

"Why, a feller hardly has to work for a living. There's food for the taking growin' on nearly every tree. Hogs aplenty everywhere, whenever you get a hankerin' for meat. With everything so easy, a man's tempted to get plumb lazy.

"Which I did. For a good long time, Othello and I just took it easy. Lazing around on the beach, shadin' up for a nap now

79

and then, wanderin' forest trails and climbin' up them big mountains they've got there. Keepin' company with them cute hula girls—who didn't interest me much, by the way, what with me still heartbroken over the fair Princess Crystalline. Ever' now and then we'd hitch a ride on one of their little boats and try another island on for size—they got a whole string of 'em. Anyway, it was a life of leisure and we was just enjoyin' it."

"How 'bout them cows?" someone asked.

"Yeah, Rawhide, you said somethin' about cattle."

"I'm comin' to that. Now, where was I? I got to noticin' that in some places on them islands there was lots of cow critters. And all them pigs. They even had free-roaming herds of scrub ponies all over the place. Which set me to thinkin'. See, the Sandwich Islands are way, way out in the middle of the ocean, thousands of miles from anywhere and nowhere. So, I says to myself, how did those critters get there? I knew they couldn't all be strong swimmers like that horse Othello, so where did they come from?

"I got to talkin' to some of them Hawaiian folks that live on those islands. Seems all that livestock got there aboard ships sailed by the Spaniards and the English and who-all, way back when. Longer time ago than anyone could even remember. They'd dump off a few from time to time on their voyages so they'd have a supply of meat out there in the ocean when next they sailed into the neighborhood.

"Well, them island folks had no use for cattle or horses. Even the pigs was mostly ignored, though the people did develop a taste for pork and some right fine recipes for cookin' it up. But them pigs hung around the villages so they didn't take no work. Anyway, with food ready at hand at every turn, it just didn't make no sense for them people to start up in the cattle business. Which means the herds grew and grew. And I'm here to tell you, them cows grew in some mighty strange ways."

"How d'ya mean?" someone asked.

"Big. Some of them mother cows was the size of a horse. And, of course, the bulls was bigger still. And seeing as how they spent a lot of their time making their way through thick forests on thin trails, their horns—which was mighty big—quit growing outwards like a normal cow critter and started growing frontways. They'd just grow out of the front of their heads and point straight ahead. Some of them even curlicued around one another until they were almost one horn. Looked sort of like one of them unicorns you read about."

"That the truth, Rawhide?" Enos wondered.

"Sure as I'm born."

"*?>+#@^&!" McCarty said.

"I'm telling you boys, that's the honest truth. And them cows was plumb ornery. Being so oversized, and not having anyone to handle them, they got to where they thought that island belonged to them. Some places, they was so cranky that folks didn't dare walk through there. Them cows would chase them down those forest paths, proddin' them along with them big ol' horns. Time to time, they'd stampede through a village and knock down them grass huts folks lived in, tear up all their belongings, and scare off all the dogs. Some villages ended up abandoned entirely, and the people canoed over to other islands to live.

"Anyway, after a time I got plumb tired of bein' lazy and tired of seein' them wild cows pester those people, and I decided to teach them cattle some manners—and maybe start me up a ranch of sorts while I was at it.

"First off, of course, I needed saddle stock, so I catched me up a bunch of island ponies and took the rough off them, then taught some of them Hawaiian boys how to ride—can't tell you their names, on account of them people have names as long as a rawhide reata. So I just named them Pineapple One, Pineapple

Two, and Pounder, which was a name they give to big waves that hit the beaches over there. And that boy was as big as a wave, I'll tell you. I figured he'd be handy at groundwork when it come time to handle them cattle.

"Then we built us some fences out of these skinny trees they call bamboo. Stuff grows like grass over there. Ain't no bigger around than a cinch ring but stronger than post oak.

"Next thing, of course, we started rounding up cow beasts. Which wasn't no picnic. A man'd get beat plumb to death chasing them out of the trees, and often as not they'd duck back into the forest before you could get them penned."

"Why didn't you just rope 'em, Rawhide?" a cowboy asked.

"Like I told you, them cattle's horns grew frontways out of their heads. They was easy enough to get a loop on, but it would just slip right off when you got them turned for a heel loop. And them horns was so long you couldn't hardly swing a big enough loop to get deep enough for a head catch. But, finally, I invented a new kind of shot where a good roper—such as I am, as you all know—could figure-eight that loop around that antler and the end of the nose. Later on, I got so good at it that I never even needed a heeler to catch their hind legs. I'd just flip that figure-eight a little deeper and wrap up their front legs and they'd be caught, but good, and would just lay right down for you.

"Me and Pineapple One and Pineapple Two and Pounder would neck them cattle to trees and leave them to think about it for a day or two, and we soon enough had cows tied up all over that island. Then, of course, we'd turn them loose and gather them into them branding pens we'd built.

"You've all been to brandings, boys, but you ain't never seen the likes of that event. Pineapple One and Two, who I taught to rope and who took to that twine like they was born with one in their hand, would drag the cows to the fire. Pounder, and a passel of his pals who was as big or bigger than him, would tip them over and hold them while I laid the brand on their hairy hides.

"But here's the interesting part. Havin' so many cattle to handle, I knew we'd need a plenty big fire to keep the irons hot. So, we gathered a big ol' pile of wood and stacked it up on a mountaintop in the middle of the island, where it would be handy to all them brandin' corrals we'd scattered around the country, and we lit a match to it.

"We kept brandin' and brandin', and that fire kept burnin' and burnin'. I'll tell you, boys, that fire was so hot that pretty soon it started melting right down into that mountain."

"Melting? Melting what?"

"That mountain. You see, it was pretty much solid rock when we started, but that fire finally got so hot it started in to melting that rock. Turned it plumb liquid, we did.

"$)&>#!"

"It's the truth, I'm telling you! And that fire just kept on melting down deeper and deeper, until there was a big hole down the center of that mountain plumb full of boiling rock. Bubbling, it was, like a pot of beans. Pretty soon that melted rock started spittin' out the top of that hole, and seepin' out cracks on the sides of the mountain. Some of it would cool off pretty soon and turn back into rocks, but some would just keep on flowin' along like a slow river, all the way down the mountainside, across the beach, and right into the ocean.

"That stuff was so hot it would just burn its way through the trees. Wasn't no way to stop it and nothin' to do but get out of the way. Made quite a sight after dark, it did. Glowing bright red and orange and yellow and white—why, it'd light up so bright you could see it for miles around. And what a ruckus it raised! Hissin' and spittin' and poppin' and cracklin' like nothing you ever heard of before."

"All that from a brandin' fire?" said Arizona.

"Absolutely true."

"*@#$?+!" McCarty said.

"I wouldn't lie to you boys. We plumb melted the whole inside of that mountain. And so far as I know, it's still a-boiling away over there. Turned into a regular tourist attraction, they say. And scientists from all over the world show up there to study it.

"But that's neither here nor there. Me and Pineapple One and Pineapple Two and Pounder managed to get a brand on all them cattle and put them on pasture. They got plumb docile, too, especially all them wild bulls we turned into gentle steers. Didn't trouble or trample folks no more, and quit their hostile ways. Made it so eating beef wasn't hardly any work at all, which, as you might imagine, improved those folks' diets considerable.

"Them Hawaiian boys took to cow and horse raisin' like they was born to it, and pretty soon there was big ranches all over them Sandwich Islands. All it took was someone to show 'em how it was done. That someone, of course, bein' me."

Said Enos, "So what happened next?"

"I don't suppose it's any surprise that I was quite a hero in those parts. The king and queen adopted me into the royal family—which might have come in handy in my wantin' to hitch up with Princess Crystalline of Eurostandovialand, what with me being a royal myself now. But, too little, too late, I suppose.

"Anyway, once them Hawaiians got the cattle business well in hand, I decided it was time for me to head east and get back to the West I was accustomed to. First chance I got, I took passage on a sailing ship and came on home.

"Only sad part of it was leaving Othello there on them islands. But I figured his fancy bloodlines would improve them scrub ponies they had over there, so I left old Othello behind to live a life of leisure, luxury, and love. He'd earned it, after all, what with swimmin' me across that ocean and all.

"That Othello was the best horse I ever rode, I do believe. 'Course even the best horse can't hold a candle to a bull moose when it comes to coverin' the country," Rawhide offered as he hunkered down into his sougans and lowered the brim of his thirteen-gallon hat over his eyes.

"Moose? Whaddya mean by that?"

"Not tonight, boys. I gotta get some shuteye," Rawhide Robinson said.

"(&?/:=#*!" McCarty said.

CHAPTER THIRTEEN

In which Rawhide Robinson witnesses the birth of the Teton Mountains

"You boys ever hear of Jackson Hole?" Rawhide Robinson asked as the cowboy crew tucked into another ordinary meal of bacon and beans and biscuits.

"Sure, I heard of it," Enos said. "Somewheres up there in the Wyoming country, ain't it?"

"Ain't that the place where them Teton mountains are?" Arizona said.

Said Rawhide, "That's the place, boys. It's a sight to see, it is. The Tetons are about as beautiful as mountains get. The thing is, they didn't always look like they do now."

"How's that?"

"Well, you look at that mountain range now, it's all jaggedy and pointy, with these big, steep peaks stretching all along the west side of that valley, or 'hole' as the fur trappers used to call it. Time was, though, and not so long ago, the Tetons looked more like a butte or a mesa. You boys know what I mean—it sloped up pretty steep from the Idaho side to a more-or-less flat top, then with steep and deep cliffs dropping off into Jackson Hole. You know what I mean; more like the plateaus and mesas a fellow sees everywhere around the Western country, rather than them peaks that look like they belong in the Alps of Europe."

Rawhide mopped the last of the sop off his tin dinner plate

with his last bite of biscuit and dropped his dishes into the washtub. But he kept his coffee cup after dumping the dregs and refilled it. The rest of the crew followed suit, more or less, each completing the suppertime ritual and settling in to see what might develop in the way of the evening's entertainment.

Once relaxed, Arizona said, "I saw a likeness of them Teton mountains in a picture book once. Looks like the kind of mountains a feller would want to go around, rather than over."

"True enough," Rawhide said. "The Jackson Hole side of them mountains is mighty steep, and there ain't hardly no way to get down if you're up there, or up there if you're down. But, like as I said, they didn't always look that way. And I'll tell you why.

"One time I was in Idaho just riding around seein' the country, and decided to take me a look at Jackson Hole. So I rode on up to the top out on that high plateau that used to be there where the Tetons are now, just to have a look at that beautiful valley I'd heard so much about.

"And pretty it is, boys, what with piney woods and clear lakes and miles of meadows growing grass, and sage flats spreading around, and that big old Snake River meandering along through it all. And sittin' up on top there, where I was, a man was so high above it was like lookin' at a great big map.

" 'Course being up that high, you lose all perspective."

"Per what?"

"Perspective, McCarty. Means bein' able to see the relationship among things, relative size and distance and such like."

"&*@?#+!" McCarty said. "Leave off with the fifty-cent words. What's that got to do with anything, anyway?"

"What happens in a situation like that, when your perspective gets all fouled up, is that what you think you're lookin' at ain't what you're lookin' at at all."

Confused faces ringed the fire, all with both eyes affixed on

Rawhide Robinson.

"The thing is," he continued, "that Jackson Hole is isolated, more or less cut off from the rest of the world. So the flora and fauna there—"

"The what?"

"Flora and fauna. Plants and animals. Trees and bushes and critters and such. Anyway, being on their own like that, in that lonesome valley, what with it being such a rich and fertile country, well, things grow big. Bigger than you can imagine. Only thing is, you don't know it looking at it from a distance. Which I was, sittin' up there on that mesa or butte or whatever you want to call it, lookin' down.

"Come to find out—which I did find out later—what I thought was ordinary elk a-grazin' down there was twenty, thirty feet high at the shoulder. Sage hens, which was thick as fleas on a hairy sheep dog, by the way, was big as a fat steer; land sakes, you could feed a roundup crew for two days on one of them chickens. And a little old bushy-tailed squirrel in that country was of a size that a fellow could throw a saddle on it and go for a ride.

"(<$&★@#!"

"It's the truth I'm telling you, McCarty. 'Course, like as I said, I didn't know it at the time and would not have believed it myself if not for what came after," Rawhide said, then paused to blow the hot off his coffee and have a sip of the thick brew.

Tension built around the fire until it threatened to start popping threads like an overstretched hemp rope.

"Well, &★@=! What happened?"

"Calm down, McCarty. I'm gettin' to it. Just give me a minute to collect my thoughts. Make sure my memories is in order." After a few minutes (which seemed like hours to the impatient drovers), Rawhide Robinson relaunched his story.

"I spent the better part of the afternoon just ridin' along atop that rimrock gazing at the amazing scenery down below there, and watchin' all the critters. There were big herds of elk wanderin' everywhere in belly-deep grass, bunches of deer browsing on shrubs and bushes, moose scattered among the willows along the streams, coyotes and wolves skulkin' around, chipmunks and squirrels and rock chucks and all manner of little critters, even saw a wolverine snufflin' about."

"Wolver what?" someone asked.

"Wolverine," Rawhide Robinson said. "They don't have them critters this far south, but there's a plenty of them up north."

"So what's one of these wolverines look like?"

"I suppose the best way to describe it is, it looks like a squatty-legged little bear. Fact is, some folks call them skunk bears. There ain't no animal in the woods as mean as a wolverine. They're braver than an animal twice that size. Why, they'll take on a bear or a wolf or a man or just about anything, and keep on fighting till the end. Usually, I'm told, they'll win the fight. Jaws like a vice that won't let go and teeth strong enough to bend the barrel of a Henry rifle, if not bite right through it. Not only that, they got claws that'll cut through cast iron. Long and sharp they are, hooked to strong, squatty legs front and back, and they can dig like nobody's business.

"So, anyway, I spent so much time up there sightseeing that I figured I might just as well make camp. Which I did. Staked out the horse I was ridin', plopped my saddle on a fallen log, built me a little fire, and stirred up some chuck. Then, after admiring the sunset, I settled in to readin' a book of poems by that English fellow William Wordsworth."

Rawhide Robinson's eyes glazed over at the memory and he paused in his telling, temporarily lost in thought.

She dwelt among the untrodden ways

Beside the springs of Dove, Rawhide Robison quoted when again he resumed the tale.

A Maid whom there were none to praise
And very few to love:
A violet by a mossy stone
Half hidden from the eye!
—Fair as a star, when only one
Is shining in the sky.
She lived unknown, and few could know
When Lucy ceased to be;
But she is in her grave, and, oh,
The difference to me!

"Why, that's right purty, Rawhide," Doak said.

"^+#@%*! Leave off with the sad poems about women or you're likely to lapse into another fit of ennui. Get back to your story."

"Hush up, McCarty," Enos said. "A little culture won't hurt you none. But he's got a point, Rawhide. What happened?"

"Sorry boys," Rawhide Robinson said. "Thinkin' about that day plumb took me right back there. Anyway, as I sat there by that crackling fire keepin' company with the fine words of Mr. Wordsworth, the ground started shaking and I could feel this rumble. Thought maybe it was an earthquake or something, but it was regular-like, like footsteps. Kept getting louder, and closer, and pretty soon I could hear some noisy snufflin' and snortin', like a hog rootin' mast. But I couldn't see anything. Yet."

Rawhide Robinson paused.

"And then!?"

"And then that wolverine I saw earlier down in that valley, or another one just like it, comes stomping out of the woods. That's when I realized I hadn't been seeing Jackson Hole in proper perspective."

"Whaddya mean?"

"Well, that wolverine was big. Real big. Remember I said

they're kind of like a small bear? This wolverine was the size of a two-story hotel, one with a saloon attached, as sure as I'm sittin' here."

">=$*&@!"

"Boys, I'm tellin' you the honest truth. Stompin' around, he was, mashin' big old boulders into gravel, snorting around and frothing at the mouth. And his eyes was all shiny-like, glowin' orange as a campfire. I knew right off somethin' wasn't right. I figured that wolverine had the hydrophoby, and I believe it to this day.

"Anyway, he come out of them woods swingin' his head side to side, trailing long threads of frothy drool, tipping over trees and snapping them like toothpicks. That horse of mine was in a panic, but it didn't last long on account of that wolverine ate him. Didn't even take a bite. Just snarfed him up and swallowed him whole.

"I figured I was next, so I lit out of that camp on the run with that big old wolverine hot on my trail. But beings as I was so small, and his eyesight being affected by that hydrophoby, I was able to elude him. He'd leap to where he last saw me and claw out chunks of that plateau, chomping and biting out pieces the size of a small mountain and spitting them back out.

"We run from one end of the country to the other, me always able to keep one step ahead of him or duckin' out behind him, and him chewin' up the countryside like nobody's business. I was tiring out after a while but that giant hydrophoby wolverine showed no sign of givin' up and I knew I had to think of something fast.

"So, on the next trip past my campsite I got me an idea. There was my kack, sittin' there on that log where I'd left it. Well, boys, I swung into that saddle and aimed the whole works downhill into this snow-filled crevice. See, that country is so high up that in some places the snow don't ever melt but packs down into ice. They call them places glaciers, and, lucky for me, that was one of them.

"So, there I was, a-slippin' and slidin' and floatin' and flyin' down that ice chute towards Jackson Hole, with the sound of that hydrophoby wolverine ripping things up still in my ears. That trip was worse than any bronc ride I ever been on, boys. Trying to keep in the middle of that log and staying upright whilst shootin' down that chute tested my saddle skills something awful.

"Anyway, after what seemed about a week, but couldn't have been more than an hour or two, or maybe a couple of minutes, I bottomed out in Jackson Hole. It was still the dead of night and I couldn't see much of anything, so I snuggled up under a tree to await the sunrise. And when that sun came up, boys, I was in for the surprise of my life.

"Like as I said, that country is so rich in that valley that everything grows big. Real big. I first noticed it in the grass, as I had come to rest at the edge of a little meadow. Them blades of grass was tall as an ordinary pine tree and thick as McCarty's head—"

"#@+<*~!"

"—Why, a man could cut a ton of hay out of two blades of grass—but it would take a company of lumberjacks to put it up rather than a crew of hay hands. And the shrubs and bushes was the size of trees, and the trees as high as the sky.

"And the animals! Heavens to Betsy, boys, you wouldn't believe the size of them critters in Jackson Hole. What, from on high, had looked like ordinary elk and deer and mountain goats and such was actually the size of city buildings. Birds big as freight wagons and fish long as a barbwire fence. It was a sight, I'm here to tell you.

"I slung my saddle over my shoulder and set out exploring that country, not knowin' what I was going to do but knowin' I had to think of something, as I was in a fix. 'Course I had plenty of stuff in my saddlebags to see me through a day or two. But, before long, I'd have to find my way back to civilization. It was mighty tempting, though, just thinkin' about loungin' around that country and livin' off the fat of the land. Till winter, that is. I did not doubt that winters in Jackson Hole would be mighty fierce.

"Anyway, there I am wanderin' around having a look-see and finally made my way across the valley and looked back at where I'd come from. And, lo and behold, I got my first glimpse of that high country where that hydrophoby wolverine had taken after me.

"That ornery critter had chomped and clawed chunks of that mesa away until there wasn't a flat spot on it! Now it was all ragged, jagged peaks poking up in the sky. Why, you could even see the teeth and claw marks! I'm telling you boys, you ain't never seen the like of it. I guess that's why them Tetons looks so different than other mountains thereabouts—or anywhere-abouts—it's all on account of a hydrophoby wolverine."

Enos laughed. "I heard of the Tetons, Rawhide, but I confess I ain't never heard how them mountains came to be."

Arizona laughed. "Now that you mention it, that picture book photograph I seen of them mountains did sort of look like big old snaggly teeth, or something teeth took a bite out of."

McCarty snorted. "*&@#+! I ain't never heard such a load of codswallop. But I suppose we might as well hear the rest of it."

"Well, there ain't much more to tell," Rawhide Robinson said. "And it bein' past my bedtime, I'm not inclined to tell it tonight."

"Aw, c'mon, Rawhide," Doak said. "You can sleep when you're dead. Tell it!"

"Not tonight, boys. I'm ridin' off to dreamland. I'll tell you about my trained moose some other time."

"Trained moose?"

"★&@#+∼!" McCarty said as Rawhide Robinson tipped his thirteen-gallon hat over his eyes and almost immediately started snoring.

With a smile on his face.

CHAPTER FOURTEEN

*In which Rawhide Robinson trades a trained moose for
a dancing horse*

The cowboys rolled out slowly the next morning, yawning and drowsy, suffering from lack of sleep thanks to last night's later-than-usual storytelling session, where all sat wide-eyed under the mesmerizing spell of Rawhide Robinson. And so they met the day slouched in the saddle, inattentive and weary-eyed.

But half-closed eyes snapped wide open when the first shots rang out.

The weariness of the crew led to a lack of alertness, which resulted in a sorry band of unscrupulous rustlers stealing up on the herd unnoticed. There were four of them, riding out of the morning sun at a dead run, guns a-blazing. Angling into the herd, scattering startled cattle in their wake, they separated some two hundred head out of the bunch and stampeded them westward.

Enos Atkins, scouting around about a mile ahead of the herd, heard the shots, quickly assessed the situation, spurred up his mount, and beat a trail to cut off the path of the stolen cattle. As trail boss, his very livelihood depended on delivering those cattle to the railhead. Letting rustlers run off with part of the herd would have personal economic consequences, as well as causing a wound to his pride that would be slow to heal. So he rode hard, and he rode fast, and he pulled his Winchester saddle gun from its scabbard on the way.

Back at the herd, Rawhide Robinson, though an ordinary cowboy with no rank over the others, just naturally took charge of the situation if no other reason than experience had taught him how best to handle such a state of affairs. He shouted for McCarty and another young cowboy riding drag to ride hard along either side of the herd to discourage any more steers from following the stolen cattle or bolting the other direction. He sent Doak and two other hands hard after the fleeing rustlers and their plundered herd.

On his own—being an experienced herder like Rawhide— Arizona and the other point rider turned the lead steers away from the fleeing animals and kept pushing them, with help from Rawhide and another flank rider, into a slow mill, with an eye to stopping the herd and holding the upset animals there.

Once the cattle were gathered and calm, Arizona lit out on the rustlers' trail; Rawhide Robinson would follow. He told the other four cowboys to stay with the herd and ride circle to keep them bunched.

Three started riding as instructed. McCarty did not.

"&%#@*+, Robinson," he said. "Who died and made you trail boss? I intend to go after them cow thieves. You stay here and babysit these steers if you want, but I'm for going."

"No, button, you're not. You'll end up getting yourself or someone else shot and I won't have it. Do as you're told."

"{*^?#*&! I don't take orders from the likes of you." With that, the young cowboy unholstered his revolver and pointed it at Rawhide Robinson.

Unimpressed, the older cowboy rode toward McCarty and struck the crown of the boy's hat a sharp blow with the rawhide quirt tethered to his wrist. Before McCarty even knew it was happening, Rawhide Robinson reached out and jerked the six-gun from his hand.

"Now you listen to me, boy. Enos and Doak and them might

be in trouble out there. I ain't got the time to sit here and listen to your chin music. So you just keep these critters from runnin' off till we get back and you can take it up with Enos. Or me, if you'd rather. I'll be happy to pin your ears back once I've got the time."

With that, Rawhide Robinson handed the pistol back to Mc-Carty, wheeled his mount and lit out across the plain, leaving the red-faced boy in his dust.

By the time he arrived, the party was over. The stolen cattle were bunched, some even lying down to recover from the run. Arizona, Doak, and the others were riding out to fetch the few stragglers and strays. Rawhide could see Enos across the way, dismounted and squatted before a man sitting flat on the ground. Seeing the cattle well in hand, Rawhide rode around the bunch and joined the trail boss.

He reined up in time to hear Enos say, "You know, old man, you ought to be old enough to know better."

"That's true enough," the man said as he raised his bowed head. Rawhide saw under the brim of the big hat that he was, indeed, an old man. Had fifteen years on Rawhide, if he had a day. That, or ten years of hard living.

Enos had ripped the man's shirt open, and he held a wadded-up bandana in the hollow between the outlaw's collar bone and shoulder. Blood seeped around the edges of the gory rag, but the wound didn't look serious enough to cause much concern. "Man your age ought not be out stealing cows and getting shot at."

"That's true enough too."

"Hold that rag right there," Enos said, and got up and walked over to his ground-tied horse. He pulled his canteen from the saddle horn and offered the old bandit a drink, which he accepted.

"You won't be dyin' today," Enos said. "Leastways not from

that bullet hole. But I could hang you from the wagon tongue right now and be within my rights."

"That too is true enough. But you gotta know that I wouldn't be stealing your cattle if I could see any way around it. I won't bore you with the story. Suffice it to say I've come on hard times and when a couple guys in a saloon invited me in on this deal, I saw it as a way to get back on my feet.

"I'm hoping you won't hang me. But I won't beg. If you opt to string me up, why, I suppose I'll just have to play the cards I've been dealt. I won't hold it against you none."

Enos hung the canteen back on his pommel and swung into the saddle. "I guess I ain't in a killin' mood today. You tell your pards to stay away from this herd or I'll shoot every last one of you on sight. We'll be takin' these steers back to the herd. I don't care which direction you go, so long as it's the opposite one of what I take."

With that, he rode away.

Rawhide Robinson, from his perch in the saddle, contemplated the old man sitting below. "You're a lucky man," he said.

"That's true enough. But right now, I ain't feeling so lucky, out here on this prairie as I am, afoot and leaking blood."

"Your horse is out there somewhere. If he's any kind of good, he won't have gone far. Maybe them other thieves will come and fetch you."

"I doubt that. Don't hardly know them. And they sure don't care nothing about me. I wasn't lying when I said this was nothing more than a crime of opportunity for me."

Rawhide Robinson rode away, feeling some sympathy for the man and his plight. But not much. Rustlers just weren't worthy of it, plain and simple.

He took up a position moving the recovered steers back to the herd. The cowboys pushed the steers into the resting cattle and used the momentum to get all the animals on their feet and moving up the trail. There were hours of daylight remaining and still miles to make, and, to Enos's way of thinking, an altercation with outlaws was not worthy of any more delay than it required.

Supper was a silent affair that evening, as the cowboys had missed lunch making up for lost time. So the cook had driven on and parked the chuckwagon a normal day's drive up the trail. When the crew finally arrived for supper, they crawled off their horses hungry.

Wisely, McCarty said nothing to Enos concerning his encounter with Rawhide Robinson. Nor did he say anything to Rawhide. But, as the saying goes, if looks could kill, the young cowboy would already be standing over the old cowboy's corpse.

Rawhide Robinson didn't give it a thought, allowing Mc-Carty the satisfaction of his hatred.

Once the ordinary meal of biscuits and beans and a few cups of hot coffee were inside them, the relaxed cowboys asked Rawhide to carry on with last night's tale.

Enos said, "I'll allow it, but only if it don't take long. I don't want another batch of half-asleep cowboys saddlin' up again tomorrow morning. Them rustlers might make a return appearance, and I want all you boys to be alert and on the lookout."

Rawhide Robinson topped off his coffee cup and settled onto his bedroll, back propped against his saddle in the ordinary way. He fussed and fiddled and finally picked up the thread of the story.

"So, boys, you'll recall that there I was, unhorsed in Jackson Hole with my saddle on my shoulder, having escaped the savage attack of a hydrophoby wolverine and survived a reckless sleigh ride of sorts on an icy glacier down a steep Teton mountainside.

"Being born to the saddle, I wasn't partial to walkin' out of that valley packin' my own saddle. But I couldn't see no horse herds around. Which is a shame, what with all the feed there is in that country. Now, I could have saddled up an oversized bushy-tailed squirrel or one of them colossal chipmunks, but, well, you know, a man's got his pride and ridin' a rodent was a bigger disgrace than I could countenance. Worse, almost, than walking.

"Finally, I saw a big old mama moose knee deep in a bend of the river munching on whatever it is mama mooses munch on. And there on the riverbank nearby was a baby bull moose takin' a snooze and soakin' up the sun. So I got me an idea that I might could ride that baby moose. I dropped my saddle and proceeded to let out the cinches and latigos full length, on account of that moose, even being a gangly little baby, was bigger around in the girth than a plow horse by a whole bunch.

"Then I proceeds to creep up on that moose, seeings as how if that moose was to wake up and stand up, I wouldn't never be able to hoist my old saddle high enough to get it perched atop its spiny back. Well, it worked, but just barely. Soon as that old kack landed, that baby moose was on its feet, spinnin' around and bellerin' and wonderin' what kind of parasite had taken up residence on its topside. It was all I could do to get the latigo through the cinch ring, pull out what little slack remained, and get hitched into a hole, what with bein' flung all over the place and using up most all my strength and ingenuity just keepin' aholt of that critter.

"Once I was cinched down I climbed hand-over-hand up the side of that moose and found the seat of my saddle. By now, as you might imagine, that mama moose was wonderin' what was happenin' to her baby.

"She come-a-runnin' out of that water with blood in her eye, but was so flabbergasted by what she saw she just more-or-less froze up. I suspect she had never encountered such a situation before, and had no instinct to tell her how to respond. So she didn't. Just stood there like she was nailed down, save for a lot of pawin' and snortin', and watched me jaunt away on her progeny."

"Her what?"

"Progeny. Offspring. Issue. Descendant."

"+<}@*$#!"

"Baby, McCarty. Her baby."

"Whyn't you just say so."

"I did. Said progeny. Perfectly good word."

"&~+^%!"

"Hush up, McCarty. Rawhide, tell it. Talk on."

"All right, then. Where was I? Right. So, there I was, aboard a baby moose with no way of knowin' what was to happen next. I figured the only thing there was to do was hang on and ride out the storm. That moose never bucked or anything like that; I guess jumping and kicking don't come natural to a moose. But that beast did a passel of twistin' and turnin' and twirlin' and whirlin' and spinnin' and stoppin' and startin' and stampedin' like there was a bolt of lightning buzzing its backside every step of the way.

"Finally, that oversized ungulate started to tire, so I unstrung my lariat, shook out a loop, dropped it over that moose's head, twisted a half-hitch over its snout, and strung it back to make reins of a sort. Never could teach that moose to neck rein, but soon enough I could crank on that makeshift rope rein like the lines on a buggy horse and get that big old baby to turn as pretty a circle as you could want. You could cut a figure-eight and he'd change leads nice as you like.

"It's quite a ride, aboard a moose. Sort of like riding one of them fancy-gaited horses they got back East and over there in Europe. Walkin' didn't come natural to him, so he went pretty much everywhere on the trot. I could quirt him into something resembling a lope, but that moose spent as much time movin' up and down as forward, which was a pretty wild ride.

"And, I swear, boys, when that moose got in a hurry it took to pacing! Now, that was a pretty smooth ride as to its up and down motion, but it did twist and turn a fellow's spine.

"Downright tiring, ridin' a moose.

"And noise! There ain't no way you could go anywhere unannounced on that moose on account of it must have had twenty-three sets of dewclaws on each one of them long legs, and they all rattled every step of the way. Sounded like a hogshead half-full of pea gravel rolling across a railroad bridge. Good thing I didn't have to sneak up on anybody while aboard that moose."

Rawhide Robinson rested from his ruminations and refilled his coffee cup, leaving his audience to contemplate the outcome of the adventure. They allowed the raconteur to nestle back into his sougans before urging continuation of the tale.

"Well, boys, there ain't much more to tell. I just pointed that moose downstream and followed the Snake River right out of Jackson Hole. And, I don't mind tellin' you, I cast many an admiring glance at them Tetons as we traveled, right proud of the part I played in their comin' to be. Anyway, the river ripped and roared down a narrow canyon, then turned right through some rolling hills and set into meandering across a big empty plain. After a while—few days, it was—we come to a settlement on the river called Eagle Rock."

Said Arizona, "So what did folks there think about a cowboy ridin' a moose?"

"They was a mite curious, I'll give you that," Rawhide said. "By then, I'd had enough of moose wrangling and was hankerin' to get back aboard a horse, but I couldn't find anybody willing to trade."

"So what happened?" Doak asked. "You sure weren't ridin' a moose last I saw you, so you must of got rid of that critter some way."

"Here's what happened. I lounged around Eagle Rock for a time, workin' at the livery stable and tendin' stock at the stage station, barely earning enough for my keep and not knowin' how to get out of town.

"Then one day a traveling circus came through there. Now them folks was quite intrigued at the prospect of a trained moose. Right up them circus folks's alley, that sort of thing. So we worked a trade—them takin' that moose, and me getting' a trick horse from their show in exchange. I did manage to get a bag of popcorn and a show ticket to boot, but it was a more-or-less straight-across trade.

"Kept that horse for a couple of years. White as snow and right pretty. Good traveler, he was. Which ought not be a surprise, seein' as how he spent all those years on the road with that circus. Got to where he was pretty good at working cattle, too.

"But then I took this job on a ranch down in Arkansas that was run by this old cowboy from Australia—only, according to that fellow they don't call them 'cowboys' down under where he come from, they call them drovers.

"Those Aussies have a lingo all their own, to hear them tell it. 'Stead of broomtails, they got brumbies. Cow ranches are called cattle stations. Pastures are paddocks. Open range is the outback, or sometimes the bush. And so on."

"C'mon, &#%@ it!" McCarty said. "Ain't nobody cares nothin' about no Australia. What about that horse?"

"Well, here's the deal. Them Aussie cowboys are right handy with the stock whip, and they use it all the time while herdin' cows, or even horses. That old feller could pop a blue-tailed fly off a heifer's eyelid and never ruffle an eyelash. Right smart with that stock whip, he was.

"Anyway, every time that cow boss popped that whip, that white horse of mine would rear up on his hind legs and paw at the sky, then drop to all fours and take to high-stepping along in a fancy little dance. Something left over from his circus days, I suppose, as they used whips in their training and shows. So, it was no fault of his own on account of he was taught that way. But it surely did raise havoc with cow work, I'll tell you.

"Lucky for me, there was a cowboy on that outfit that was young and feelin' his oats, and thought that trick horse would be just the thing to impress the local school marm. See, he was tryin' to convince that young lady to step out with him and figured a fancy dancin' horse would give him the edge over all the other men who was trying to turn her head. So he took that trick horse off my hands and I was back to ordinary old cow ponies.

"Which suits me just fine, me bein' an ordinary cowboy and all," Rawhide Robinson said as he snuggled down into his sougans for some much-needed shut-eye.

CHAPTER FIFTEEN

In which Rawhide Robinson sleeps on a feather bed

If there's one thing there's aplenty of on a trail drive, it's kinks and twists, knots and tangles. And not just in lasso ropes. What with all the hard riding after bunch quitters, the jolts of the quick turns of a cutting horse, and just plain hours and hours in the saddle, a cowboy's bones get a mite misaligned.

And a night's sleep doesn't always offer relief. Fact is, on occasion it makes it worse. Sleeping on the ground offers little comfort to begin with. And it seems like every rock, stone, and pebble in the vicinity irresistibly migrates to an uncomfortable spot under a cowboy's bedroll. And, even wallowing out a hip hole doesn't make a bed of grass and soil much more accommodating to the human form.

So, after a week or three on the trail, every cowboy's fitful sleep is punctuated with dreams of freshly laundered sheets, fluffy comforters, a soft pillow, and a tick stuffed to overflowing with feathers. And, sooner or later, such yearnings inevitably come up in campfire conversation.

"Oh, what I would not give for a night in a feather bed," Doak said one evening after supper. "Right about now I could snuggle down into a soft mattress and sleep a week."

"I'm with you on that," Arizona said. "If I close my eyes, I can almost feel it."

"~$+#*@! There ain't no feather beds around here, so you might as well shut up about it. Waste of time even talking about it. Toughen up, you bunch of boobs."

Arizona said, "Well McCarty, you're young yet, and your body ain't bothered so much by sleeping on the hard ground every night. But just you wait. You get some age on you and you'll be dreaming of feather beds yourself."

"%*&>{! There ain't no point even thinking about it. Ain't never been no feather bed on no trail drive, and there ain't never going to be one."

Silence descended on the campfire crowd, the cowboys disheartened by McCarty's dismissal of their dreams, his reminder of their ongoing discomfort, and his harkening of a continuing lack of relief. Finally, though, as is often the case, the quiet was interrupted by Rawhide Robinson.

"You know, McCarty, that just ain't so. Why, I myself have slept on a feather bed many a night on the trail."

"Nonsense. That ain't nothing but another one of your *&)@%?# lies."

"Hold on there, boy," another cowboy said. "Let Rawhide speak his piece."

Said another, "C'mon, Rawhide. Tell us about it."

"Well, here's the deal," Rawhide Robinson said. "It was on a trail drive some years ago. We was holding a herd in Indian Territory, waiting for a permit to cross into Kansas, when this wagon train came by and circled up just upwind of the herd, as any wagonmaster with a lick of sense would do. Anyway, he meant to stop there for a while to recruit his teams.

"Thing was, this wasn't no ordinary wagon train of sodbusters going west. It was a freight train, hauling, of all things, a load of chickens. Laying hens, they was. Seems some fellow out in the mining country somewheres in southern Nevada took a notion to get rich selling fresh eggs, fryers, and stewing hens. So he ordered up a herd of chickens and had them freighted out to him. It was a fortuitous turn of events, I'll tell you—"

"Four, two, what?" McCarty interrupted. "+/]@#! As usual, Robinson can't just say what he means."

"Fortuitous. Means a happy accident," Rawhide Robinson explained. "You know, something unexpected, but good."

"*%=<! Enough with the language lesson. Just get on with the story."

"Well, having all them hens in the neighborhood provided a pleasant change in menu. Our old dough roller had a field day with all them fresh cackleberries—"

"%\<#+!"

"Eggs. Eggs! Coosie whipped us up scrambled eggs, fried eggs, omelets, soufflés, French toast, soft-boiled eggs, hard-boiled eggs, flan, quiche, eggs Benedict, huevos rancheros, custard, egg salad sandwiches. . . . I'll tell you boys, it was a culinary delight there for a day or two.

"Then, one night in the dark of the moon, someone stole into that wagon camp and smashed up all the cages and turned loose all the chickens. Nobody ever figured out who or why, but there were chickens scattered across the plains as far as the eye could see.

"That wagonmaster enlisted our aid, figurin' if we could round up cattle we ought to could do the same with his scattered hens. Well, with us not engaged in any cow work to speak of at the moment, we thought to give it a try. And, strange to say, it worked. Sort of. We did have to modify our methods somewhat."

"How do you mean, Rawhide?"

"Well, you couldn't rope one, for one thing. We soon enough learned the neck on a chicken is too scrawny to withstand a pony settin' up with the other end of the lariat tied to the saddle horn, or even when you let it slip some with a dally. Heeling them didn't work much better. Even the best ropers among us was unable to jerk the slack quick enough to keep the loop from slippin' off them skinny little legs. And you couldn't push them chickens like you can cattle. Try to ride into the hip of a hen like you would an uncooperative steer and before you know it you've ridden right over the top of it.

"Most of all, though, we had to learn to use our chaps."

"What?"

"As you know, chickens ain't much for flying. They can't get too high nor go any distance. Still, they can fly some. And that caused considerable problems when trying to herd them hens. So we'd strip off our chaps and carry them across our laps, and when a hen would try an airborne escape, we'd just swat it out of the sky. It might have addled their brains for a minute, and a few might sprain an ankle if they took a hard landing, but there was no lasting damage and it worked pretty good.

"Anyway, we rounded up all them hens and pullets and held them on a bed ground while them freighters nailed up some new cages. But, as it turns out, chickens are birds of a nervous and sensitive sort. All that excitement had upset 'em, and all them hens went into a molt and started shedding feathers all over the place. Which wouldn't do no harm to the chickens so long as the weather didn't turn off cold. But, anyway, all them feathers just layin' around gave us an idea.

"Every so often, we'd send a crew out to gather up all the feathers, leastways the soft ones. And we fashioned ticks out of our bedroll tarps and stuffed them with them feathers. I'll tell you, boys, that made for some mighty fine sleepin'. Of course them mattresses was a bit thick and bulky, which presented a challenge when it was time to move on up the trail.

"But, big as they were, they weren't much heavier than air, so we worked it out. Figured out we could just stack them, one atop the other, in the hoodlum wagon and they'd ride along just fine. Quite a sight it was, that wagon lumbering along with that big, tall stack of feather beds stickin' up in the sky and rockin' back and forth. Sure made it easy to find the camp, though. Like a sentinel on the prairie, that stack of mattresses was."

"*&@#%$%!"

Rawhide Robinson rose from his bedroll on the hard ground and refilled his coffee cup. But, after settling back into his nest in his sougans in his ordinary way, he showed no intention of continuing.

"So is that it? That's the end of the story?"

"Who cares? Ain't nothing but a pack of &*#$ lies anyway."

"Stuff it, McCarty. What happened next, Rawhide?"

"Well, boys, things went along without incident for a while, and we surely did enjoy the comfort of them feather beds. But one day a twister came along. Big whirlwind—you know the kind—one of them that'll rip off your clothes and blow the hide right off of you.

"We all survived it, us and the cattle, but it ripped our feather ticks all apart and sucked them feathers right up the funnel. Then, the darndest thing happened—them feathers started falling out of the sky like snowflakes. A lot of snow. Why, boys, it looked like a serious snowstorm out there on that prairie, even if it was July."

"@#$*&!"

"It's the honest truth, McCarty. Feathers floating around everywhere. We all had to tie our bandanas over our mouths to keep from sucking in them feathers and strangling. But that ain't the worst of it.

"See, them cattle, they thought it was the real thing—a genuine, no-kidding, Katie-bar-the-door snowstorm. So they sulled up right there where they stood and refused to move another inch. Them feathers kept fallin' and that whole herd just stood right there shiverin'. By the time them feathers was a foot deep, them cattle had plumb given up. Froze to death, they did, right where they stood. Every last one of them."

"?/&+=@!" said McCarty. "What a lot of nonsense."

"Nevertheless, that's the truth of it," Rawhide Robinson said as he slid down into his bedroll and tipped his thirteen-gallon hat over his eyes.

"But when it comes to cold, that weren't nothin'. You remind me sometime, and I'll tell you boys what *real* cold is."

And with that, Rawhide Robinson drifted off to sleep, dreaming he was once again comfy and warm, tucked into a feather bed.

CHAPTER SIXTEEN

In which Rawhide Robinson spends a hard winter on
the Northern Plains

The moon was high and nearly full, washing the prairie with pearlescent light. The temperature was moderate, the air fresh and clean. No matter how one looked at it, it was, in every way, a delightful night to be horseback.

Still and all, despite the congenial circumstances, Rawhide Robinson was his usual melancholy self while riding night guard. Never mind that he was a man whose daytime disposition was bright as the sun. At night, while circling the herd, his mood tended to darken with the sky as memories of lost love and other of life's disappointments leaked into his thoughts, displacing his ordinarily cheerful and carefree character and countenance.

So, as Rawhide Robinson rode along through the beautiful night in a blue funk, a soft tune floated out from the space between his bandana and thirteen-gallon hat, and filled the air with a glum miasma.

> *From this valley they say you are going.*
> *We will miss your bright eyes and sweet smile,*
> *For they say you are taking the sunshine*
> *That has brightened our pathway a while. . . .*

He crooned quietly as he rode.

So come sit by my side if you love me.
Do not hasten to bid me adieu.
Just remember the Red River Valley,
And the cowboy who loved you so true. . . .

He continued.

The music infiltrated the subconscious depths of the crew, affecting the attitudes of all. No one knew why, but everyone awoke in a mood subdued, if not downright saddened, by the gloomy tune. They went about their trail-drive tasks quietly all that next day, and conversation around the campfire that evening was nonexistent.

Trail Boss Enos Atkins recognized the downhearted disposition of his cowboys, and, in fact, felt it himself, and realized the need to lighten the mood.

"Say, fellers," he said. "What say we sing a song? A little music might brighten things up around here a bit. Rawhide, lead us in a tune."

And so he did.

Unfortunately, his song selection was misguided. Without knowing why, he launched into the tune lingering in his mind from last night:

From this valley they say you are going.
We will miss your bright eyes and sweet smile,
For they say you are taking the sunshine
That has brightened our pathway a while. . . .

And the cowboys around the campfire joined in automatically, for that particular melody had, unknowingly, permeated their memories as well:

So come sit by my side if you love me, they sang.
Do not hasten to bid me adieu.

Just remember the Red River Valley,
And the cowboy who loved you so true.

Alas, the singing did not accomplish the trail boss's purposes. Despite all their best efforts—the cowboys tried singing harmony parts; they attempted the song in the round; sang duets, trios, and quartets in various combinations; some hummed while others sang; they even composed verses of their own to add to the song—the music did not lighten the mood.

If anything, in fact, things got worse.

"%^+>*@!" McCarty said of a sudden. "Enough of this! If I never hear that miserable song again it'll be too soon. Robinson! Tell us a story."

Immediately, instantly, surprise—shock!—displaced melancholy. Every cowboy around that campfire was rendered speechless by their young saddle pal's request.

Rawhide Robinson, likewise dumbstruck, stuttered and stammered and finally spat out a refusal.

"Not tonight, boys. I just ain't got it in me."

"C'mon, *~+$#! Usually we can't shut you up! Tell us all about how you was elected king of Siam or some other such nonsensical nonsense."

"Well, I'd be right happy to tell you about that, only except no such thing ever happened. And, as you boys know, I never tell anything that ain't the honest truth."

McCarty would not be dissuaded. "Well, &#@&*, tell us something! Anything!"

Other cowboys joined in until the encouragement became coercion. As one always willing to please, Rawhide Robinson eventually relented.

"Let me think," he said, stalling for time. And he stretched the delay by refilling his coffee cup, rearranging his bedroll, stirring up the campfire, and adding fodder to the flames. But, still, nothing came to him.

Finally, Doak said, "Rawhide, after you told us about them cattle freezin' to death in that hen-feather blizzard, you allowed as how you'd tell us sometime about *real* cold. Remember that?"

"Why, thank you, Doak. I reckon I do remember. Now, let me see," he said as he settled onto his sougans in the ordinary way, adjusted the saddle at his back for maximum comfort, and wet his whistle with a sip of scorching coffee.

"One season, rather than signing on with a crew to drive steers to Kansas for shipping east, as I ordinarily do, I took a job driving a mixed herd way up north to the Dakota Territory, where this wealthy combine of eastern and European money intended to found a cattle empire. Ours was just one of several herds they contracted for, having purchased cattle from Texas, Arkansas, California, Indian Territory, Utah, Oregon, even Mexico, and who knows where all else.

"By the time autumn arrived—and it comes mighty early up north—there was cattle spread all over that country. Of course they needed cowboys to run that ranch, such as it was, being mostly just open range, so me, not havin' anything else on my plate at the time, signed on.

"Which, as it turned out, was one of the biggest misadventures of my life."

Rawhide Robinson took another moment to collect his thoughts, then carried on.

"Things went along fine, for a while. I was assigned to a line camp out near the Black Hills, which is mighty pretty country. The grass there grows pretty good, and them cattle was doing fine. Me and the boys in the bunkhouse hadn't much to do, just easy ridin' during the days, checkin' on the cattle and keepin' them from driftin' towards the badlands.

"Then one day all of a sudden it turned off cold, with this howlin' wind that I swear was comin' straight from the North Pole. But wherever it come from, it was packin' plenty of chill with it. A man couldn't put on enough clothes to keep warm.

"Next thing you know, it started in to snowing. Them flakes fell down, they fell up, they fell sideways, and every other direction there is. Made that hen-feather storm look mild by comparison. Why, you'd go outside to the privy or to fetch firewood or to feed hay to the horses and come back plastered with snow on every side, lookin' like a drawing of a snowman in a picture book. It was so cold, boys, you couldn't hardly even ride. Fact is, we'd have to burn the barn down every morning just to thaw out the horses."

"$<&~*#!"

"Now, all that would have been fine for a day or two. But it just kept up, on and on, day after day, for weeks on end. Seemed like it wouldn't ever stop. Snow piled up and drifted till the cows couldn't get to no feed. Buried them Black Hills so deep it covered over all the trees, which was worrisome on account of our firewood was running low.

"Which didn't make all that much difference, really, because it was so cold the heat from that little cookstove and the fireplace we had in that line shack didn't provide any warmth at all. Why, sometimes, late at night or early in the morning, the fire itself would freeze right up."

"%)#$!>!"

"It's the truth, boys. Them flames would quit flickerin' altogether, and just hang there in the air like orange icicles. You'd have to take a stick of wood and knock them around a bit, stir them up a little to get them burnin' again. Otherwise, they'd just dangle there in the air and do no good whatsoever.

"Boys, it was so cold you couldn't even drink coffee. Why, you'd pour it out of the pot and it would freeze solid before it hit the bottom of your cup. All we could do was break if off in chunks and eat them like they was coffee-flavored popsicles.

" 'Course it was worse at night. When the fire would burn

down or freeze up, why, it got so cold a man's snores would freeze up in midair and wouldn't make no noise at all. I admit I enjoyed the peace and quiet, rooming with a bunch of heavy snorers like I was. Leastways I would have enjoyed the quiet if I had been warm enough to enjoy anything.

"Of course, them frozen snores didn't stay frozen. Once we'd get the fire stirred up or it'd warm up a bit in the daytime, why, they'd all thaw out at once and raise a ruckus like you wouldn't believe.

"All them snores goin' off at once—a whole night's worth in just a few minutes—would rattle the rafters and practically blow that line shack right off its foundations. I imagine they could have heard it clear down in Amarillo if the wind was right."

"^&*@#$!"

"Hush up, McCarty," Enos said. Then he asked, like any cow boss would, "What about the cattle, Rawhide? What happened to them in all that cold?"

"Well, Enos, it was a mixed bag. Them that froze up down in the draws and gullies and coulees and got drifted over with snow just stayed froze up till springtime, then thawed out and did just fine. The ones caught in open country didn't fare nearly so well. Oh, they survived it, but we lost most of them anyhow."

"How's that?"

"Here's the thing. They'd be froze solid, just standin' out there in the snow and doin' just fine—till the wind would come up. Which, of course, it always would, the Dakota Territory being nearly about as windblown as any place can be and still stay put.

"If it got to be a stiff enough wind, why, then, them stiff critters would just blow away. We'd see them going by all the time, just rolling across that frozen prairie like tumbleweeds.

"Now and then, they'd drift up in the lee side of a little ridge, but mostly they'd just tumble on out of sight. We rode out in the spring looking for them, and gathered some, but there just weren't no tellin' how far south they'd got to.

"I imagine as they got much farther south, down to where it was warmer, they would have come unfrozen and wandered off anyway—heading south toward the sunshine, if they had any sense."

"Well, how 'bout you? How'd you-all survive it," Doak wondered, "you and them other cowboys?"

"We did all right, all things considered," Rawhide Robinson said. "We had plenty of grub, when we'd get enough heat to get it cooked. The worst part came when we ran out of firewood."

"Whatever did you do about that?"

"Like as I said, our cow camp was near the Black Hills, so we had cut and laid in a good supply of firewood. Enough to last any winter. Except that one, as it turned out. And, like as I said, the snow was so deep on them mountains that there wasn't no sign of no trees—no hide nor hair of any tree, anywhere. Every tree in that whole country was buried under deep, deep snow. Except for one.

"A ways out on the plain, a little bit west of them mountains, was this big old lone tree. You could see that thing for a hundred miles in any direction. I'll tell you, that big old pine tree was taller than any tree I ever seen or heard of. Taller, even, than them giant redwoods and sequoias out there in California I told you about.

"We hated to go to whittling on that tree, seein' as how it was so useful as a landmark; sort of a guidepost out in that country, if you know what I mean. Folks of all kinds, Indians and trappers and traders and travelers and all, used it to get their bearings. But, we were given no choice if we wanted to keep from freezing plumb to death.

"So we went to chopping on that tree, and it took a good many days just to make a dent in it. But by workin' in shifts we eventually tunneled through, then hacked our way out toward one edge until that big old tree tipped over. Now, you boys may not believe this, but it's true nevertheless—that tree was so tall it took it seven days and a night to hit the ground once it started falling.

"*#+@#!"

"Told you you wouldn't believe it. But it's the truth. Now, as you might imagine, it would have been a heck of a job to cut a tree that big into stove wood. Thing is, we didn't have to. It was so cold that even that big old tree had frozen all the way through, so when it hit the ground it shattered. Busted itself up into chunks just the right size for burnin' in a stove or fireplace.

"So, needless to say, we was well fixed for firewood for the remainder of the winter. Fact is, that tree had enough wood in it to provide firewood for everyone in that country for years to come.

"Why, folks would just ride out in a wagon and pretty soon they'd come across a cord of firewood stacked nice and neat out in the middle of the prairie where there wasn't a tree in sight. Most folks never had any idea about why it was there or where it come from. They'd just load it up and haul it on home and write it off to good fortune."

McCarty said, "^&@?*! That's as big a barrel of hogslop as I've heard in all my born days! Ain't no way no such of a thing ever happened."

"Wrong again, boy. It happened just like I told it. And the proof is right there for anyone who cares to see it."

"%*@]+! What kind of lies are you telling now? What proof?"

"You don't have to take my word for it, McCarty, since you ain't inclined to anyway. Just get on your horse and ride on up there. Like I said, it's just a ways west of the Black Hills, just outside the Dakota Territory in Wyoming. You can't miss it."

"Miss what?"

"The stump of that tree. You see, that tree stump stayed froze solid all through that winter and got so hard it turned into solid rock, with the bark still on it and all. Why, it's a thousand feet high if it's an inch. They even got a name for it—call it Devil's Tower."

"&@?/>#!"

CHAPTER SEVENTEEN

In which Rawhide Robinson rides the river

Another ordinary day on the trial, another ordinary adventure for Rawhide Robinson and the cowboy crew.

This day, yet another river flowed across the intended path of the herd, which necessitated another crossing. The stream was slow-moving and sandy, wide, but not deep, and the biggest hazard it posed was troublesome quagmires of quicksand that could catch a steer by the legs and refuse to let go.

And so the cowboys spent a bone-wearying day in mud and water, encouraging and aiding bogged steers to pry themselves loose from the swampy, sucking sand and mud and plod on to dry land.

Some of the cattle were easy to pull loose. A loop around the horns, with the other end of the rope tied off or dallied to a saddle horn, and a steady pull by a stout cow pony would allow the struggling steer to work its way out of the mud and onto firmer footing. Others, however, sunk ever deeper into the shifting sand with every move. And that required a hands-on approach.

One particularly difficult incident saw a steer up to its withers in the river, half of which, from the tops of its front legs on down, was thick, soupy mud. The hind end of the animal was bogged even deeper. The steer had struggled there for some time while the cowboys freed others, and had given up the fight. Now lackadaisical and apathetic, it appeared resigned to living out the remainder of what would be a short life sinking slowly into oblivion.

But, cattle being the currency of their trade, the cowboys were determined to save every steer. And so Rawhide Robinson had the critter roped by the horns, supported in the struggle by another young cowboy from the crew. In the muddy stream with the steer were Doak and McCarty, afoot, and nearly afloat.

One on either side of the bogged steer, the cowboys, mud-coated to the tops of their Stetson hats, lifted and strained, tugged and twisted at the animal and its parts and appendages. Reaching down to the river bed and beyond, they grasped and groped at hoofs and hocks, flanks and fetlocks, legbones and dewclaws, pulling and prying, lifting and twisting, attempting through their concerted efforts and the strain of the ropes to free the steer from the sucking mud.

"$%@*!" McCarty said, spitting mud and venom with every syllable.

"I do believe I feel some movement on this hind leg," Doak said, blowing the occasional bubble as he spoke, straining to keep his head above water.

"&%+~! I think this leg is gettin' deeper every second."

Rawhide Robinson shouted, "Boys, try locking arms behind his hocks and lift together."

And so they did. Arms entwined around the steer's hind legs, shoulders pressed against its rump, they boosted the beef with all the strength they could muster. And then McCarty lost his footing. He went down, muddy water flooding over him. Arms flailing, he rose out of the water spitting and sputtering, grit in his teeth and sand grating the insides of his eyelids.

"%<#@*!" he roared.

Rawhide Robinson couldn't help but laugh.

"*+~%}!" McCarty spat with a spray of muddy water. He grabbed Rawhide's rope and started hand-over-handing his way toward the giggling cowboy. Rawhide backed his horse a few steps, allowing slack in the rope, then jerked it forcefully, popping the lariat out of the young cowboy's hands and laying a welt along his cheek in the process.

"You just turn yourself around and get back to work," Rawhide Robinson said.

"&#(>@?/!" McCarty said. "%#*!"

"If you're of a mood to lay hands on someone, make it that steer," Rawhide Robinson said. "Get back down that rope and get to it. Not now—right now!"

Reluctant but resigned, McCarty turned and waded back into the deeper water, taking off his saturated hat and swiping it at a smiling Doak. The young cowboy's anger renewed his strength, however, and he clawed deep into the water and wrenched a hind leg free, then another, then twisted the steer's tail as he and Doak again locked arms and bodily lifted the animal out of the bog.

The ropes stretched from the steer's horns shivered with tension, and, slowly, the waterlogged critter tipped forward, pulled a front leg free, then another, and pawed and struggled its way out of the muddy stream and toward the riverbank as if suddenly remembering that staying alive is preferable to a permanent nap under the mud.

Once ashore, Rawhide rode around the steer, wrapping his rope around its hocks and, with the other cowboy keeping tension on its front end, used the leverage of the lasso ropes to lay the animal on its side. Squishing and squirting water out of soggy boots with every step, Doak grabbed and bent the steer's front leg back and squatted against its soggy hide with a knee on the animal's neck and the other in it ribs while McCarty loosened the now-slack lariats from the horns.

The steer stood up, shook like a wet dog, and trotted nonchalantly toward the herd as if today were nothing more than another ordinary day in the life of a cow critter.

As it happened, that was the last of the trapped animals and the crew lined out the herd and pushed it on up the trail until reaching the place Enos had chosen for overnighting.

It was a damp evening around the campfire, as all the cowboys had been saturated from the knees down, some drenched as high as the chest and shoulders, and a few, like McCarty, dunked altogether. They sat close to the fire, some peeling off wet boots and spreading moist clothing to dry. Others rotated themselves in the fire's heat like a pig on a spit. All especially enjoyed the ordinary fare the cook ladled onto their plates, seasoned as it was with fatigue and hunger, and appreciated even more the scalding coffee in tin cups almost too hot to hold onto.

After a while, as ordinarily occurred around the campfire, relaxation dampened down the cares of the day and the cowboys sought the distraction of a song or story. It was Arizona, this time, who stirred up a story from the embers of Rawhide Robinson's memories.

"Oh, this river was quicksandy enough," Rawhide Robinson said. "But, sure, I've seen worse. The worst I've encountered wasn't on a trail drive but occurred one time while I was working a ranch job down in New Mexico.

"Come to think of it, it wasn't so much being bogged in the river that was so troublesome as what happened after."

After waiting a suitable interval for the raconteur to assemble his thoughts, Doak spurred the story ahead.

"Well, what? Tell us about it."

"Here's the long and short of it, boys. You've all heard, I reckon, of that part of New Mexico around Fort Sumner. That's where the infamous outlaw—or gallant young cowboy, depending on who's telling the story—Billy the Kid got caught up in that so-called Lincoln County War between the Tunstall and

Chisum interests in livestock and commerce."

"&%$+!" McCarty said. "Now you're tellin' us you knew Billy the Kid?"

"I ain't tellin' you no such thing. I was nowhere near New Mexico when all that nonsense recounted in them dime-novels occurred. What I am sayin' is that part of the country is where this here story I'm tryin' to tell you took place."

"Yeah, McCarty!" Arizona said. "You just put a lid on that pie-hole of yours and let the man talk."

"Anyhow, I was punchin' cows for this outfit on the Pecos River some ways south of Fort Sumner. And one day this big old steer wandered into the river, tryin' to rid himself of flies, I suppose, and got himself bogged, but good.

"Now, the thing is, this wasn't no ordinary steer. He was old and big; big enough to pull a freight wagon over Raton Pass single-handed, unless I miss my guess. He'd put most any ox I ever seen to shame for stature and tonnage. See, that rancher kept him around for a trail steer, just like Charlie Goodnight kept Ol' Blue.

"This critter was white, but speckled so heavy he was nearly as much red. Had a set of antlers as wide as the Texas panhandle, and they took a full twist before they sharpened out to razor-thin points. Ordinarily, that steer was docile as a milk cow. But, I suspect, being stuck in the Pecos mud put him in a foul mood.

"So when I rode out into that water with a hole punched in my rope, he didn't act too glad to see me. You'd think a trail-smart old mossy horn like him would recognize I was there to help him, but he sure didn't. He was a wagglin' those horns at me and bellerin' a challenge soon as I rode up.

"I dabbed a loop on that speckled steer and proceeded to haul him out of the mud, which, as it turned out, wasn't that big a task. For some reason, he come sucking out of there slick as axle grease. But that did not improve his mood any, sad to say.

"And that was when the fun got underway.

"See, I rode up on that ornery critter to pull my rope off his horns. But just as I reached down to snag that reata, why, he turned tail and headed downstream at a high lope. He hit the end of that rope, and I'll tell you boys, I parted company from the cow pony I was aboard so fast you could hardly feel the jerk, and, lo and behold, I was still a-sittin' in my saddle. That cinch had turned loose and so there I was, both feet in the stirrups, backside holding a deep seat, flyin' down the Pecos River as fast as that steer could scamper."

As was his wont, Rawhide Robinson paused in the telling to allow tension to build, filling the studied pause with seemingly ordinary tasks like topping off his coffee cup, straightening his bedroll, and shifting his saddle so as to construct a more comfortable backrest.

McCarty could stand it no longer.

"*&?#@, Robinson, get on with it!"

"I will, McCarty, I will. Don't get your underwear in a bunch."

But, still, the storyteller took his own sweet time settling in and carrying on.

"Now then, where was I, boys? Oh, I remember—I had just set sail down the Pecos River deep-seated in an un-cinched saddle with a lariat tied to the horn, the other end of which was looped around the horns of an ornery, oversized, speckled steer.

"Now, here's the thing about the Pecos River thereabouts. It runs—leastways is did back then—straight as a string and pretty much due south. Why, a fellow could fire a rifle up or downstream in that river bed and the bullet would be over water its entire flight, and splash down in the middle of the stream when spent. Nary a bend in that river for miles.

"Well, here's what changed that. That steer must have been spooked by whatever he was draggin' behind him—that 'whatever' being me, as you recall. So he took to duckin' and divin' down that river, veering left then right, then left again.

"With every turn and bob and weave, I and my saddle got to whiplashing farther and farther out to the sides, bouncin' up and down on that river like a stone skippin' over the surface of a smooth lake. Then, pretty soon, I got to flyin' and slidin' out over the riverbank, farther and farther out, and we got to plowing into the soil and rocks and dirt along one side of the river and then the other. And each time I'd hit, I'd gouge out a big old trench, turning the earth like I was a human plowshare. Then, of course, everywhere that steer and me had plowed a new channel, why, that river water would rush right in, carving out a new course as it went."

">+@~*#!"

"It's the truth, McCarty, and the evidence is there to see. You take a look at the Pecos River down there a ways south from Fort Sumner, New Mexico, and you'll see that it meanders through that country as crooked as a sidewinder snake. Why, there's twists and there's turns, there's oxbows and there's loops—that river is anything but straight, as anyone who's seen it will swear to."

And with that, Rawhide Robinson tipped his thirteen-gallon hat over his eyes and settled in for a good night's sleep.

And McCarty, as was wont with him, stewed and fussed and bubbled and boiled inside until steam practically shot out his ears.

And, as had become ordinary on this particular trail drive, anyone there could have predicted that another story, on another night, would again raise the young cowboy's temperature.

And, had one been able to see Rawhide Robinson's face, you would have noticed just a hint of a smile there.

CHAPTER EIGHTEEN

In which Rawhide Robinson encounters foul weather

Despite the difficulties in crossing the boggy river, the crew—and especially trail boss Enos Atkins—was grateful to have made it across yesterday, as when they awoke buckets of rain poured down, which would have meant a swollen river and greater danger to man and beast.

And so the herd raised no dust that day as the cowboys lined them out and up the trail, the makings of dust having been saturated with the rain and turned to mud. The cowboys rode along disconsolate, wrapped in slickers to shed as much of the precipitation as possible.

Still, water would wend its way under a collar and run down the center of a cowboy's back, causing a quivery chill. Raindrops puddled in the crowns of their hats, flowed down to the brims, and created tiny waterfalls, which cascaded to the seats of the saddles to soak through trousers and create a most uncomfortable ride. Water flowed into boot tops, saturating socks, and chaps—whether tanned leather or woolies—sponged up rainwater and grew heavy on the legs.

The steers plodded along through mud and water, their hooves splashing and flinging up the sloppy soup to paint legs and bellies. Muzzles dripped drops, streams flowed from saturated tail switches, curtains of drizzle ran off slippery horns.

The horses, too, suffered the consequences of the soaking rain, carrying not only their usual load of tack and man, but all the water both could soak up as well. Cow pony ears drooped in an attempt to keep rain from filling the holes. Once-firm footing became slippery and uncertain.

"^&@+=/#!" the young cowboy McCarty could be heard to say by anyone within earshot.

Later, the wind came up and made matters worse.

Every nook and cranny, every crack and crevice, every wrinkle and fold that had managed to stay dry heretofore now soaked up moisture from the horizontal storm.

And the hands kept the herd moving up the trail, as there was no alternative. Some imagined the comfort of a career selling ribbons and sundries and notions in a mercantile establishment with a tight roof. Others wondered if they weren't better suited to counting money and toting up sums as bank clerk at a desk in a dry, warm building. A few thought of giving up the trail, turning in their time, and lighting out for more comfortable environs.

But, such is the life of the ordinary cowboy going up the trail and it does no good to grouse about it.

Except in the days of Noah, all rainstorms eventually wear out before everything floats, and so did this one. By the time the herd was bedded on high ground only slightly less soggy than the low-lying terrain, coosie had a camp established and was hard at work rolling out biscuits under a leaky canvas fly at the tail end of the chuckwagon while wet wood smoked in camp and cookfires. The wrangler had the remuda in a tight spread, cropping mouthfuls of damp grass.

All was again back to more-or-less normal, only wetter than usual.

"$*#>@!" McCarty mumbled as he stomped—squished—into camp, soggy saddle on his shoulder and mud dripping from his batwing chaps.

"I'll agree with you there," Arizona said. "This is about as much misery as a man can stand."

"It's mighty painful, all right," Doak agreed, and most of the other cowboys in the crew lent support to the notion that this day had been about as miserable as a day could get.

"Oh, pshaw," Rawide Robinson said. "I'll agree with you that today weren't no picnic in the park. But as bad weather goes, this didn't amount to much."

"Oh, ^%@)*/, Robinson," McCarty said. "I suppose you're going to tell us another one of your cockamamie tales."

"Not if you don't want to hear it. But should you choose to further your education, check back with me after supper and I'll see to your enlightenment concerning foul weather."

The cowboys drank double portions of coffee that evening, imagining that heat from the inside would force out the cold and wet. They settled in with a final cup and one of the crew asked Rawhide Robinson to relate his experience with storms, as promised. McCarty, of course, feigned indifference.

"Well, I can tell you about a deluge of rain that made today's downpour look like a spring shower," Rawhide said. "And I will. But first off, boys, I'll tell you about the strangest storm in my experience. Not strange as in unheard of, but unusual in its effect on me.

"I was ridin' circle on a roundup on a big ranch in the Indian Territories. A Cherokee outfit, it was. Clouds started rollin' in like waves on the ocean; every shade of gray you can imagine, all the way to white and black. Then the air started buzzing like a swarm of bees and turned yellow and green. Lightning flashed all around, and them thunderbolts rollin' through the air liked to've knocked me plumb out of the saddle.

"When that horse I was mounted on started fidgeting, I knew we were in for trouble. He spread his legs and squatted down a-quivering like a cryin' baby. Wouldn't move an inch no matter what. Then this big old white tail dropped down out of them clouds, wagging back and forth like a dog saying he's glad to see you. I wasn't glad to see that cyclone coming, I'll tell you.

"That funnel cloud hit the ground maybe three furlongs away from where I sat that horse, and commenced to rippin' up chunks of sod the size of washtubs and rolltop desks and flingin' them around in the wind as if they were cigarette papers. That wind kept whippin' harder and faster, and that tornado hoppin' and skippin' all over the place, and there wasn't a thing I could do but watch.

"Then that twister jumped up in the air and dropped down right over the top of me. Strangest place I have ever been, inside that thing. Wind whippin' around us so fast you couldn't see through it, but it was still as Sunday services there in the middle where me and that horse was. Then we started liftin' up off the ground, and me and that horse took to spinnin' around—but real slow-like.

"As we moved across the prairie, we kept gettin' higher and higher up inside that thing, just driftin' along, floatin' through the air like we didn't weigh no more than a dead leaf off a scrub oak. And all around us, out there where the wind was blowing hard, there was every imaginable thing flying past. Saw tumbleweeds. Trees. Jackrabbits. A jersey cow. Why, there was even a homesteader's soddy going around and around."

"^$+#@&!"

"It's the truth, McCarty. And that ain't the half of it. The longer we was up there, the more stuff that twister sucked up. Saw three horses—a bay and two pintos—a whole passel of longhorn cows, a Hereford bull, and the dome off some state capitol building, although I cannot say which state.

"There was corral rails, pine planks, baled hay, a bathtub. Even saw a buckboard and a Studebaker wagon whirlin' around. A litter of pigs. Posthole digger. Hens. Turkeys. Barn cats and cow dogs. More things than I can recollect.

"Can't say how long me and that horse rode that whirlwind, but it seemed like a month of Sundays. Finally, though, that whirling started slowing down bit by bit, and took to droppin' off rubbish here and there. Set me and that horse down gentle as you please in fetlock-deep grass.

"Once the wind died down I could get a look around, but that country didn't look familiar. Found out later we was in southeastern Missouri somewhere."

"*★^$=@$!" McCarty said. "There ain't no way no such a thing could happen."

"And yet it did. And that ain't all."

"What?" asked Arizona.

"Say it," a cowboy said.

"Well, here's the thing of it," Rawhide Robinson said. "That tornado had laid out all that debris it was carrying and arranged it just so. Fact is, the way it was arranged made it so I found myself sittin' on a horse in the middle of a ranch headquarters that had not been there before the storm. The whole outfit, see, was built by that cyclone. Corrals with solid posts and tight rail fences all around. Barns and outbuildings all assembled—made out of mismatched wood, you understand, but well built and waiting for a coat of paint. Right tidy place, it was."

"&★@#!"

"Strangest thing, though, McCarty, was the ranch house. That wind planted that capitol dome right where you'd want a fancy house. And I reckon that was about as fancy-a-looking house as you could ask for.

"And, of course, there were horses in the corral and cattle in the pastures. Chickens in the henhouse, turkeys in the barnyard, pigs in the pen. All courtesy of that tornado."

"I suppose you laid claim to the whole #$%^& outfit and became a gentleman rancher," McCarty said.

"The thought did cross my mind. But before I even had time to dismount, here come a white-top buggy down the lane with a real-estate salesman aboard and a couple of fobs from back East in the back seat, totterin' atop their fat wallets. I saw right off the way of things, so just rode away."

"*^%+>~!" McCarty said. "At least you didn't get rained on like we did today."

"I'll give you that. Not that time, anyway. But did I ever tell you boys about the time we got caught in the rain out on the Red River?"

"No, %$%#@<. But I got a feeling you're about to."

"Button your lip, McCarty," Arizona said. "Talk on, Rawhide. Let's hear it."

"Well, there we was, holding a herd in a big bend of the river waitin' out a storm. It had been pourin' down rain for two or three days before we even got there and it showed no sign of lettin' up. We dug in there, as we had no choice but to wait for the river to recede so's we could cross.

"But it showed no sign of doing so as the rain kept comin' down like singletrees and butter churns. It was so wet ducks set off waddlin' toward higher ground and bullfrogs sprouted wings and took to flyin' away.

"Well, all that hard rain started gnawin' away at the very soil, with washouts all over the place. Before you know it, the river started eroding away its banks, tightenin' up the loop we were in, just like a roper jerkin' his slack. Before we could move the herd, the river cut through the narrow end of the bend and all of a sudden we were on an island. We figured we had to just sit it out, lacking any alternative.

"Then, the Red started undercutting the banks all around us and that heavy rain kept washin' them down from the top side. In the middle of one night we was all awakened by the oddest feeling that the earth was moving underneath us. None of us had a clue what was happenin' but we darn sure knew something was up.

"Come morning, we realized all that rain and high water had cut our island loose and washed it away altogether, and that whole big patch of land with us and all them cattle was now floatin' downstream."

"&*@#!" said McCarty. "Now you've gone too far, Robinson!" he said.

Doak said, "Stow it, McCarty. I want to hear the rest of it."

Rawhide Robinson used the interruption to refill his coffee cup and allow the cowboys who wished to, to top off their own. When all were once again settled in and attentive, he again took up the tale.

"Those of you who know your geography can imagine what happened next. We rode that island on downstream to the Red River's confluence with the Mississippi—"

"Con what?" McCarty asked.

"Confluence. It's where two rivers join up, flow together. In this case, the Red and the Mississippi."

"Well, ^&#@, whyn't you just say so? You and them fancy words of yours."

"Nothin' fancy about it, McCarty, and they ain't mine. Just plain English is all."

"@#$+!"

"Hush up!" Enos said. "Let the man talk."

Rawhide Robinson said, "Where was I? Oh, yeah. So there we were, floatin' along down the Mississippi River like Huckleberry Finn, only except our raft was made of a big chunk of Texas, or what used to be part of Texas, 'stead of logs and lumber.

"We finally run aground around about New Orleans, tied off that island, and called it good. Had quite a time in that city, we did, me and the boys. And that's the end of that story," Rawhide

Robinson said.

"Now hold on there a minute," Enos said. "What about them cattle?"

"Whatever do you mean, boss? They made the trip same as we did and arrived in the Crescent City in fine fettle."

"I get that. But most every trail herd that left Texas in them days was headed north, most for the railroad in Kansas. There, most cattle boarded trains bound for Chicago, then points east in the form of beefsteaks, chops, ribs, and roasts.

"Unless I miss my bet, the man ramroddin' that outfit you were with had a contract to deliver that herd to a buyer in Kansas, if not to market in Chicago."

"Well, of course you're right, Enos. We did end up in an altogether different place than was intended. But, thanks to the glory of that telegraph outfit they got in them civilized places like New Orleans and Chicago, we got it all sorted out.

"So, instead of reachin' Chicago aboard train cars out of Kansas, them misplaced cattle were loaded onto steamboats and hauled to Chicago in luxury and high style."

"$%(~!" said McCarty.

"Shut up," said Enos. "At the rate we're goin', this herd of ours ain't gonna get to market on a steamboat or any other way. You boys had best turn in. We got miles to make up tomorrow."

"G'night, boys," Rawhide Robinson said.

"~@$^*+!" McCarty said.

"Go to sleep," Enos said.

CHAPTER NINETEEN

*In which Rawhide Robinson confronts hostile Indians and falls
down a rabbit hole*

The hands lined out the herd under early-morning slate-gray skies. Another day on the trail would take them deep into Indian Territory, the empty, untracked grasslands between Texas and Kansas where the presence of white men was still but passing fancy.

Just as the sun pushed its way over the eastern horizon, bluing the sky and sending a wave of yellow light rolling across the plain, trail boss Enos Atkins raised a hand skyward, the dropping of which, accompanied by a loud "Ho!" would prompt a chorus of hollers, a jangle of spurs, the slap of coiled lariats against chap-clad thighs, and start the locomotion of thousands of cloven hooves.

But, instead of signaling the start of another's day drive, the trail boss trotted his eager mount toward the tail end of the herd, eyes locked eastward, squinting into the glare of the rising sun. Each cowboy relaxed, sagged in the saddle, and looked to see what distracted their leader and delayed the day's drive before it started. Stirred-up dust clouds cut the sun's shimmer, revealing a half-dozen horsemen pounding their way across the prairie toward the herd.

"Indians!" someone hollered, and the hands instinctively pressed closer to the cattle, ready to hold the herd against the threat of stampede.

But the Indians slowed their approach, checking their racing horses down to an easy lope, a trot, then a high-stepping walk before reining to a stop a short distance from the right flank of the herd.

Rawhide Robinson's assignment for the day was riding on that right flank. He turned away from the herd to face the visitors. Enos approached on the trot from the front; the kid McCarty, curiosity and a sense of duty overcoming the fear that dried his mouth and set his hands to trembling on the reins, rode up from his place at the rear. Together, the trail boss and the two cowboys rode out to face the waiting Indians.

The cowboys reined up a few yards from the visitors, whose leader set in to waving his arms and manipulating his hands in a most forceful and irate manner. Enos followed suit, and the histrionics continued in turn.

"What the &*@#+'s happenin'?" McCarty asked Rawhide Robinson in a strained whisper that could likely be heard in Fort Worth.

"Sign language. It's a simple means of communication developed by various Indian bands and tribes over the centuries to facilitate commerce."

"!@#$%*? Rawhide, I asked a simple question!"

"They're talkin'. Now hush, so I can listen in."

"*(%@*&."

"Here's the deal, McCarty," Rawhide Robinson said softly after a moment. "They're sayin' we're crossing their territory without permission, and they intend to confiscate the herd unless tribute is paid."

The Indian leader held up both hands and said, *"Wohaws,"* as he spread all eight fingers and both thumbs.

"Wohaw is Indian for cow, leastways among these folks," Rawhide Robinson whispered to the young cowboy. "He wants ten head."

"*$=/@#," hissed McCarty. "Not a chance. We ain't gonna do it, are we, Rawhide?"

"Hush."

Enos responded with the display of a single digit.

The Indian snorted and again flashed ten fingers.

Enos shook his head in the negative.

The Indian started signing so quickly his hands were a blur.

Enos responded with the display of a single digit.

The Indian signed some more.

Rawhide Robinson said to McCarty, "He's sayin' if they don't get the beeves, they'll come back tonight and stampede the herd and end up with a whole lot more than ten."

McCarty said, "(*@#?>]!"

The Indian signed off with an emphatic gesture.

Enos turned and rode away. Rawhide Robinson and Mc-Carty reined around to follow.

The Indians watched in silence for a moment, then, as if one, charged forward, splitting around the retreating cowboys, sliding their mounts to a sudden stop then spinning to face the cowboys in a hostile, seemingly choreographed display. Thus cut off from the herd, McCarty squirmed in the saddle, his breaths coming quickly, a shaking hand on the grip of his holstered pistol. Rawhide Robinson set one hand atop his saddle horn and the other hand atop that, his face as calm and as close to expressionless as a man could make it. Enos stared without blinking at the Indian leader.

The Indian's prancing pony danced toward the trail boss until his rider jerked it to a stop nearly nose to nose with Enos's horse. He held up eight fingers.

Enos replied with two.

The Indian flashed six.

Enos responded with three.

Five.

Four.

The Indian nodded approval.

"McCarty," Enos said. "Come here."

The young cowboy urged his horse up beside the boss's, wide eyes staring out of a white face.

"You been ridin' drag this whole drive. You know better than anybody which of them cattle is footsore and havin' trouble keepin' up. Go cut out four head of the worst of them and drive them back this way."

The kid swallowed hard. "You sure, boss?"

"Do it."

"We can take these thievin' #$(:!* Indians. Say the word and the boys'll be here on the run."

"Do it now, McCarty. Right now. Rawhide, give 'im a hand and see the kid don't try nothin' stupid."

"You got it, boss."

The two cowboys did as ordered, McCarty fighting his horse's head and muttering under his breath the whole time.

With a holler and a yell and a scream and a shout, the Indians choused their newly acquired wealth of four steers across the prairie as fast as the trail-weary cattle could run. Soon enough, they topped a slight rise then dropped down the other side, disappearing into the space between the horizon and the risen sun.

The trail boss heaved a sigh and said, "Let's hit the trail, boys. Get them dogies rollin'."

"+{@*&%," McCarty mumbled.

The evening around the campfire seemed ordinary in every respect. Except that McCarty nursed a nasty mood, dropping his saddle to the ground with more force than gravity required, banging his tin plate, kicking away any cow chip or twig or stem of grass or speck of dust or other offending obstacle in his path, and muttering and murmuring a stream of invectives that turned the air in his wake into a green haze.

Once the hands were on the outside of their supper and settled in around the campfire with coffee in hand, Doak said, "McCarty, what's eatin' at you?"

"*&@!(>]# Indians. We ought not to have knuckled under and give 'em them steers."

"You think?"

"We could of took 'em. There weren't but a handful of 'em."

Several cowboys chuckled, and Arizona joined the exchange.

"True enough, kid, but how many more do you suppose was waitin' over the rise? Could be a whole passel of them. Look around, and you'll see there ain't all that many of us."

"Not only that," Doak said, "We are in their country. Seems a small price to pay for the privilege."

"&^!~z+* cowardly, if you ask me," said the youngster.

Enos weighed in. "Ain't no sense gettin' all het up about it, McCarty. Every herd that comes through the Territory contributes a few cattle to the upkeep of the Indians. Them that don't do so deliberately, like we did, end up givin' 'em even more cattle on the sly.

"In this country, beef critters have a way of sneakin' off in the night and gettin' lost. Or there'll be a sudden stompede for no apparent reason, and, try as you might, you can't never gather up all the cattle that run off. You come up short every time. It's best to make the best bargain you can and chalk it up to the cost of doin' business."

"^&:~*&@<," the young cowboy muttered under his breath.

"He's telling the truth, McCarty," Rawhide Robinson said. "You make another trip or two up trail, like most of us has, you'll see it's so."

"Yeah, right," the kid said. "I suppose you know all about

Indians. Just like you do every other *&#@$ subject that comes up."

The old cowboy said nothing. He stared into his coffee mug as he swirled it around, as if he expected to find the answer to one of life's enduring questions spinning around in the whirlpool. Alas, his study revealed nothing. So he swallowed the coffee and nestled down into his seat on his unfurled bedroll.

He said, "I surely ain't no expert, McCarty, but I've been a party to some mighty strange dealings with Indians over the years. Why, I remember this one time—"

"—Oh, ?/+=*@!," said McCarty. "Not another one of your *&#$@ stories."

"Pipe down, kid," someone said. "Pay attention and you might just learn somethin'."

"Tell it, Rawhide," someone else said.

"Well, it happened here in Indian Territory, not too far from where we are right now, as I recall," McCarty said after taking a moment to gather his thoughts. "We was trailin' a mixed herd to stock a ranch up Montana way when a handful of Indians accosted us—don't ask, McCarty—much as it happened today.

"Trail boss on that trip was an intractable—don't ask—ol' cuss and he refused to give up any cattle, save one ol' lame cow and a young calf that couldn't take the pace. Them Indians wasn't pleased, but allowed we could pass if we'd alter our route some. Said their village was right in the path we was takin' and they did not want to pull up stakes. They showed the boss which way to go, and he agreed to it, as it wasn't much of a detour.

"After about two miles or thereabouts, we come across an abandoned prairie dog town, spread out over a quarter section or so. Well, despite the wave of anxiety that washed over us, we pressed on, as the terrain had funneled the herd onto that pock-marked prairie and there wasn't no reasonable alternative. We just took it right slow and hoped the cattle and the remuda would watch their steps until we cleared the hazard, and not bust a leg by steppin' into one of them holes.

"Well, boys, we made it through with no troubles—leastways we thought so. But we soon enough noticed the size of our herd had diminished considerably—"

"—Sorry, Rawhide," McCarty said. "I've had enough of your)+<#$@ fancy talk. Whaddya mean 'dim . . . dimin . . .' oh, #!]>*, whatever it was you said!?"

"Diminished. Means we lost a bunch of cattle. Means the herd was smaller. Means, despite our not noticin' anything untoward, a whole passel of the cow critters had disappeared into thin air."

"&@*&#!"

"As it turned out, it wasn't thin air at all," Rawhide Robinson said. He rose from his perch atop his bedroll and made his way to the cookfire, tipped the coffee pot, and splashed a serving of the stimulating brew into his tin cup. As was often his wont, the raconteur took his own sweet time getting back to his bedroll and wallowing his way into a comfortable nest. He blew at his coffee. He slurped up a sip to test the temperature and blew across the rim again. He repeated the process.

"+@^%$, Rawhide, will you get on with it!" McCarty said.

Another voice added, "I'm with the kid this time. Get on with it."

"Tell it," another said.

"Patience, boys, patience. It is a virtue, you know."

"&@+#{*," McCarty harrumphed. "What happened?"

Eventually—it seemed half an eternity to some of those gathered—Rawhide Robinson's relationship with his hot beverage settled into satisfactory and he continued his tale.

"Here's what happened. That ornery ol' trail boss sent a pair of us down the back trail to cut sign and see if we could locate them missin' critters. So away went me and an Irish-Mexican crossbreed cowboy name of Juan Carlos O'Casey. As good a hand as ever forked a horse, he was, ol' Juan Carlos O'Casey. We rode a lot of miles that day, we did, circumnavigating—"

"—What?" McCarty said. "Another one of your ^&@()* fifty-cent words!"

"It just means we rode a big circle around the country we'd crossed with the herd. Hush up and listen. Well, I'll tell you, boys, we couldn't find a trace of them missin' cattle. We even reconnoitered—means we watched, kid—the Indian village and saw nothin' suspicious.

"Anyway, the onliest thing me and Juan Carlos O'Casey could ascertain—don't ask, McCarty—was that there was a whole passel of cow tracks walkin' into that old prairie dog town we'd passed, and not nearly so many hoofprints walkin' out. Looked like a third of the herd had plumb disappeared.

"Well, we figured such a thing couldn't have just happened. So me and Juan Carlos O'Casey ground-tied our mounts and wandered around in that empty prairie dog town to see what we could see. No prairie dogs—like I said, the town was abandoned. Oh, some of them holes was occupied by other species of the mammalian and reptilian variety—rabbits was livin' in some, snakes in others, mice and lizards, that sort of thing. But most seemed empty.

"Me and Juan Carlos O'Casey got right down on our hands and knees and crawled around lookin' for clues. I saw somethin' suspicious, said 'Juan Carlos O'Casey, come on over here and have a look-see at this,' but got no response. I looked around and, lo and behold, there was nary a trace of my saddle pal! Juan Carlos O'Casey had disappeared as slick as them cattle."

"$+@%$&!" McCarty said.

"Shut up, kid," someone said.

"Tell the story," another said.

"Well," Rawhide Robinson said, "I wandered over to where I had last seen Juan Carlos O'Casey, and it appeared as if he had seen the same thing I had."

Rawhide Robinson paused to sip at his coffee and rearrange himself on his nest.

"+?/><#*! Get on with it!"

"Pipe down, McCarty."

"Tell it, Rawhide."

"Around some of them prairie dog holes was sign that showed where a cow had walked right up to the hole but didn't walk away. The soil surface was slightly disturbed, evidence of something or other—drag marks, maybe—not like there had been a struggle, see, but enough to pique one's curiosity.

"So, anyway, I got to pokin' around that hole Juan Carlos O'Casey had been studying and it appeared from the tracks that he'd crawled right down the hole. Well, fearin' for my saddle pal's safety, I decided I had better follow his trail. I made myself small as possible and slithered into that prairie dog hole like I was a snake and wriggled on into the darkness. Before too long or far, that hole opened up and I wiped the dust and dirt out of my eyes and lo and behold, there I was in one of the strangest places I have ever seen.

"It was semi-dark down there, but enough light filtered down that I could see just fine once I got used to it. Fact is, from down there, all them prairie dog holes on the surface looked like dim lanterns hanging on the ceiling, or maybe stars in the sky. Anyways, there I was sittin' next to Juan Carlos O'Casey and both of us rubbin' our eyes and dumbstruck by what we was seein'."

Rawhide Robinson's eyes glazed over as if his mind were elsewhere, lost in the story he told. He sat, lost in thought, sipping at his coffee until McCarty interrupted his reverie and

143

jarred him back to the present and his place around the campfire. He looked around for a moment, as if unfamiliar with his surroundings, and shook his head vigorously to clear the cobwebs.

"Sorry, boys. I kind of drifted back to that place in my mind."

"Well, &^!)*#, tell us!"

"There we was, me and Juan Carlos O'Casey, sittin' in what looked like a big ol' cave, only except it wasn't narrow like a tunnel, but spread out in all directions. All around us, the floor was littered with cow chips, some old and brittle and others fresh as a pie from the oven. We started wanderin' around and saw where them Indians had stacked prairie grass for hay, and dug out stock ponds here and there. Enough feed and water to keep a passel of cattle for a spell. Place was their commissary—we could see how them Indians must have just kept cattle hid-up there till they needed one for the stew pot.

"We wandered around down there in the dim for a spell and, sure enough, off in the distance a ways, just a-standin' and layin' about was all the cattle we'd lost. Some was munchin' on that prairie hay, some chewin' their cuds, some sippin' cool water from them little ponds, some just a-takin' a snooze."

"@#$%^!" McCarty said. "That's a lot of twaddle if ever I heard any!"

"Nevertheless, it's as true as the North Star. Them Indians could steal livestock slick as you please—just hide out down there when a herd came along and reach out of them prairie dog holes, grab a critter's leg, and pull it underground before it even had time to beller. Quite the clever operation, it was."

Arizona said, "So what did you do? Did you get them cows back to the herd?"

Rawhide Robinson swallowed the rest of his coffee and dumped the dregs then set the cup aside. He lifted his lid, ran his fingers through his hair, dropped the hat back down and pulled it snug.

"Well boys, we did. But it wasn't easy. Me and Juan Carlos O'Casey racked our brains till they was plumb wore out tryin' to figure how to get them cattle back up from underneath that prairie dog town."

Another pause. Another trip to the coffeepot. Another herd of anxiety-ridden range riders.

"&^@)(#, Rawhide, get on with it!"

"He's right, Rawhide. Finish the story."

"C'mon, Rawhide! Tell it!"

"Here's what happened. Me and Juan Carlos O'Casey pushed all them cattle way off into an out-of-the-way corner in that cavern where they'd be safe, then lit a match to all them haystacks. Burned up every stem of it, we did. Likely raised enough smoke that it looked like a prairie fire up top, but we wouldn't know, of course, as we was underground. Them flames naturally boiled all the ponds dry so them cows was without food and water all of a sudden.

"We wormed our way back to daylight, which there wasn't any of by now, it now bein' nighttime since we'd spent the whole day at our labors."

"*#@>#, Rawhide, get on with it!"

"Hold your water, boy. I'm just tellin' you how it happened. So, anyway, I stood guard in case them Indians showed up while Juan Carlos O'Casey beat it back to the herd to gather up the rest of the hands so's we could carry out our plan.

"You can imagine, what with them bovines bein' without food and water, that they'd get hungry and thirsty soon enough. And, as you know, being experienced with cattle as you are, that they'd be on the hunt for something—anything—to fill their bellies.

"By the time Juan Carlos O'Casey got back with the cowboys, them cows was raisin' a ruckus. Now, Juan Carlos O'Casey hadn't told the hands what was up, just that we needed their help to round up the cattle and bring 'em back to the herd. You wouldn't believe how befuddled them boys looked when they reined up in the middle of that old prairie dog town and heard all that bellerin' echoin' up out of the ground. Gave 'em the heebie-jeebies it did, sure enough. Had to hog-tie half them cowboys to keep 'em from stampeding."

"*(#@&%!"

"Hush, kid," someone told McCarty.

"Talk on," someone told Rawhide Robinson.

"By the time we got them drovers calmed down enough to explain the plan, the cattle was hungry enough to make it work. And it did work, I'm here to tell you, as smooth as the down on a duck's belly. By the time we was finished, we'd recovered every cow them Indians had made off with."

"How?"

"What?"

"+@*$!"

"What we did was have every one of them cowboys snug up his saddle cinch and make sure his catch rope was tied hard and fast to the horn, and we scattered them around that prairie dog town so they had the whole herd covered. Then each of them tightened a loop around a big bunch of grass and dropped it down a hole to dangle there where them hungry cows was. Just like ice fishin' in Minnesota it was, boys—them hungry critters would glom onto that grass at the end of those catch ropes and them cowboys would ride away and reel 'em in. Cows was comin' up out of them holes as slick and thick as sardines!"

All the cowboys laughed at Rawhide Robinson's story.

Except young McCarty.

He said, "?/^%*#@!"

CHAPTER TWENTY

In which Rawhide Robinson whets the crew's appetite

"&#%@!" McCarty said as he threw his tin dinner plate to the ground. "I'm so $%@* sick of beans and biscuits, I can't stomach another bite!"

No cowboy offered a reply to this loutish breach of etiquette, but, instead, sat in a silence somewhere between stunned and embarrassed. Finally, Rawhide Robinson broke the uncomfortable quiet.

"Chuckwagon fare does get a mite monotonous, doesn't it, McCarty? Gets so a man would kill for a taste of fresh buttermilk or maybe a bite of huckleberry ice cream."

Doak added, "Yer darn tootin'! Why, ever since you told us that story about roundin' up them chickens, I ain't been able to think of nothin' else but a big ol' plate of fried eggs. In my dreams I can almost taste 'em. I see a pile of 'em sittin' on a platter, kind of crispy brown just on the edges like I like 'em, with them plump yellow yolks beggin' for me to cut 'em open and go to soppin' with a biscuit."

Arizona said, "Me, I been thinkin' about steamed artichokes like my mother used to make. She'd set one of them funny-looking things on each of our dinner plates, and there'd be a little bowl of mayonnaise she'd whipped up fresh for dippin' and there'd be a bowl of melted butter besides. Me and my brothers would take to rippin' off them little leaves and givin' them a dunk and scrapin' off that tender meat between our teeth—oh, Lordy, I can almost taste it now."

With the floodgates now well and truly open, a torrent of culinary cravings washed over the cowboy crew. One talked of fresh strawberries and cream. Another of garden-fresh creamed peas and new potatoes. Another salivated over homegrown sliced tomatoes. Even the cook joined in, confessing his desire to sauté a mess of mushrooms in hot butter seasoned with minced garlic. And the crew was unanimous in the opinion that nothing would wet the whistle right now quite as well as would an ice-cold beer, from a bottle dripping wet with condensation.

"Well, boys," Enos said, "few more days, maybe a week, we'll have this herd delivered and you'll each have a pocketful of cash to satisfy them appetites. Not that you'll find all them fancy dishes in Dodge City—the place ain't exactly a gastronomic paradise—but at least you'll enjoy a change of fare."

"Can't hardly wait," someone said.

"Can't happen soon enough," said another.

"Can't stop thinkin' about them eggs," Doak said. "Tell us about them chickens again, Rawhide, and all them things the cook made out of all them eggs."

"Oh, ^&#@*+!" McCarty said. "Not again! Those stories are bad enough the first time, let alone havin' to hear them again!"

"Not to worry," Rawhide Robinson said. "I never repeat myself."

Doak's sigh—almost a groan—of disappointment was audible throughout the camp.

"But," Rawhide Robinson said, "strange as it seems, that wasn't the only time I enjoyed fresh eggs on a trail drive."

"Do tell!" said Doak.

"Soon as we finish up with supper."

With that, the cowboys ate with renewed enthusiasm, almost enjoying, it seemed, the ordinary chuckwagon fare. They shoveled in beans and sopped up the juices with their biscuits until the speckled enamel finish on their tin plates fairly shined. Coffee cups were topped off and the crew settled in for another tale from Rawhide Robinson.

"I told you boys about them hen's eggs that unintentionally caused such turmoil in our man Doak. Well, at the risk of further upsettin' him, that was not the only occasion upon which I was treated to fresh cackleberries on the trail.

"On this one drive to the north country, we encountered a heck of a storm somewhere in Wyoming, or maybe northern Colorado. That inclement weather was so fierce there was no way to tell exactly where we were, seein' as how the wind kept blowin' us around one way and then another. Started out with heavy black clouds, that storm did. Got to looking more like nighttime than the middle of the afternoon—that's how dark it was.

"Then it commenced to dump washtubs full of rain everywhere; drops so big they was dropping steers in their tracks. Didn't cause any lasting damage, just stunned them, but it took them cattle a while to get their bearings again after being downed by them raindrops."

"*@#+$!"

"Shut up, McCarty!"

"Talk on, Rawhide."

"Well, fortunately, that rain did not last long. Unfortunately, it turned into hail. There we was, out in the wide-open spaces with no cover or shelter in sight, being pounded to oblivion by hailstones.

"They started out the size of a garden pea, which smarted a bit when they hit, but not so's a fellow couldn't stand it. Pretty soon, they swelled up to the size of a grape, which, as you can imagine, caused a good deal more pain. Then, once you got used to being battered by grapes, them hailstones grew to the size of brussels sprouts. Getting pelted by one of them will leave a mark, I'll tell you.

"And that was not the worst of it. Them hailstones soon got to be the size of chicken eggs. There wasn't a thing to do other than crawl underneath of our horses and hope for the best. The saddles protected the horses some, and they could more-or-less tuck their heads out of the way, but there wasn't much to do for the cattle. Them hailstones pelted them pretty good, and a lot of cows got knocked plumb unconscious. Took them two or three days to get their wits about them, what with them already bein' dazed and confused.

"The only good news out of that storm is that it quit. And when it did, the cook on that outfit took a Dutch oven and an empty water barrel out on the plain and gathered up a passel of them hailstones. I'm telling you boys, not only did they look like hens' eggs, they tasted like 'em!"

"*<{@#!" McCarty said as he rose from his bedroll and bounced his coffee cup off the ground with a wicked toss in the general direction of Rawhide Robinson.

"Mind your manners, boy," Enos said. "I will brook no misbehavior in this camp."

"But!—That!—Why!—He!—%*?=>!—"

"Hush, McCarty. It don't matter none. Sit down and plug your pie hole, or I will."

"&@#*!"

"Talk on, Rawhide."

"Well, them eggs, or hailstones or whatever they was, was pretty well shook up, as you might imagine, what with falling out of the sky like that and then bouncing around on the ground. So, they were already scrambled and that's the only way we could eat them. Still, they was right tasty and a delightful break from our ordinary fare of bacon, beans, and biscuits."

"&*@#$!" said McCarty with his ordinary ire.

"Aaaaah," sighed Doak. "I prefer my eggs fried, but I've never turned up my nose at a batch that's been scrambled. You suppose a feller will be able to get fresh eggs in Dodge?"

"They've always had 'em before when I've been there," Enos assured him.

"Fine. Mighty fine. I do enjoy my eggs. I suppose that's why I ain't partial to eatin' chicken. The more chickens that gets eat, the fewer eggs gets laid. How 'bout you, Rawhide? You like chicken?"

"Indeed I do like chicken. Fried, roasted, stewed. Hot or cold. I enjoy eating fowl of all kinds, as a matter of fact. Turkey. Guinea fowl. Ducks. Geese—come to think of it, I ever tell you boys about the time out in Nevada when our lives was saved by an opportune feast of waterfowl?"

"Oh, %^&@#$! Not another one of your *&+% stories! Ain't one enough for one night?"

Enos said, "McCarty, I will not tell you again to mind your manners. Sit down and shut up. On second thought, get up and refill my coffee cup. And while you're at it, top off Rawhide's as well."

"&@+#*$&!" McCarty complained. But he got the coffee. And, in the best "Man at the pot!" trail-drive tradition, he refilled the cups of all who asked.

"Here's how it happened," Rawhide Robinson said once he sipped the foam off his cup. "We were in the Nevada desert, out there in the middle of the Great Basin, havin' just delivered groceries-on-the-hoof to the army at Fort Churchill. In autumn time, it was. The leaves would have been turning colors and fallin' off the trees—had there been any trees out there, which there ain't.

"Anyway, we was heading east on the Overland Trail when a freak storm struck. It was mighty cold, but it was the wind that forced us to hole up and wait it out. Which we did, usin' up most of our grub in the wait. When it let up we set out for Great Salt Lake City on the double, knowin' we could make it before takin' any hurt if we hurried.

"Then, another storm hit. Snowed some, got bone-crackin' cold. Then the wind started up again, all but uprootin' the sagebrush. Couldn't even take shelter in our tents, on account of the wind would just carry them away—which it did. Couldn't keep a fire goin' most of the time, but we managed to cook up a little something whenever we could, just to keep the fires burning inside. Which we did, till the grub ran out.

"So we were sitting there shiverin' one evening, along about this time of day, maybe a little earlier. The wind had died down some; enough that a man could sit upright without holdin' a boulder in his lap for ballast, but it was still blowin' up a gale.

"All of a sudden we heard this big thump, and we looked around and saw that a cowboy we called Shadow had tipped over right where he sat. Someone crawled over there to see what was up when the same thing happened to another one of our hands. Then, we started hearin' these thumps and bumps and whumps all around, and soon enough knew we were being bombarded—but by what, we did not know.

"It let up as sudden-like as it started, and we realized we had been assaulted by ducks. A few geese, as well. Figured they must have been flyin' south and got blown off course in all that wind, and got plumb wore out trying to stay airborne. Seems they just expired and happened to go to ground right there in our camp.

"~&=$%*!"

"It's the truth, McCarty. But that ain't the half of it."

"Oh, #@^#! What now?"

"Every one of them waterfowl was already plucked clean. Right down to the pinfeathers. Figured the wind must have done it—blown all their feathers plumb off."

"*$%@&!"

"All we had to do was just poke a stick in them and roast them over the coals. Which we did, soon as the wind let up sufficient enough to allow it. Saved our lives, they did, them plucked ducks and fleeced geese."

McCarty swore some more.

Most of the rest of the crew laughed.

A few thought how good roast duck would taste about now.

The boys then launched a discussion on favorites meats, each claiming his favorite—whether prime beef, delicate lamb, venison, buffalo hump, cabrito, German sausage, pepperoni, pork chops, roast turkey—was the finest comestible ever placed on a table.

Rawhide Robinson said, "I knew a man once—I suppose it's more correct to say *met* a man, as I did not really know him—who was right fond of pork, ham in particular."

"Oh, ^#*@#!" McCarty said. "Not again!"

"Put a lid on it, kid," Arizona said. "I do like ham myself. What about this fellow, Rawhide?"

"It was in California, it was. I was just ridin' along one day, on my way to somewhere for some reason, neither of which I recall just now. Anyway, I came across this sodbuster's place, a haywire outfit if ever there was one. My horse needed a drink so I stopped by the dooryard to ask permission and me and this farmer got to talkin'.

"Whilst we was chin waggin' this fat hog ambled over to the trough, and I swear that pig had a wooden leg on the near-side hind. He was right big, so I knew he had some age on him. But the strangest thing was that peg leg.

"After a minute or two of watchin' that hog and listenin' to that plow-chaser dally his tongue, I interrupted. 'How did that porker come to have a wooden leg?' I asked him.

" 'Let me tell you about that pig,' he said. 'One day my two-year-old boy was a-playin' out by the lettuce patch when he fell into the irrigation ditch. Wasn't anyone of us around to see it, and that boy would have drownded had not that hog—he was nothin' but a shoat at the time—jumped out of his pen, dove into the ditch, and hauled my baby out of the water by the nape of his neck. Saved his life for certain sure. That's some pig,' he said.

"Well, I thought on that for a minute and agreed that it was quite the feat, but asked again about the peg leg.

" 'Let me tell you about that pig,' the nester said. 'One day we was all out hoein' corn, all except our baby daughter, who weren't no bigger than a minute, and who was a-sleepin' in her cradle in the kitchen. A pine knot from a log burning in the fireplace must have popped loose and set the hearth rug ablaze. Then pretty soon the flames was licking at that child's crib quilt.

" 'Well, that pig there, he ran into the house, dumped over the water bucket to douse the fire, and taken up that baby wrapped in its blanket in its mouth and carried her out of the house for safekeepin', just in case that fire flared up again. 'Course we didn't know none of this till we knocked off for dinner and come on back to the house. And there was that baby, out in the dooryard, cuddled up next to that hog and sleeping like a—well, like a baby.'

"That story, too, gave me cause for thought, and, again, I agreed with the hoe-man that that was, indeed, an extraordinary example of porcine perfection. But, I asked again, how'd that pig come to lose a hind leg?

" 'Land sakes, man!' he said. 'You don't eat a pig like that all at once!' "

And while McCarty didn't laugh, as the rest of the crew did, Doak swore he saw a hint of a smile on the young cowboy's lips as he cut loose with a half-hearted "&^#@$*!"

CHAPTER TWENTY-ONE

In which Rawhide Robinson leaves the trees

The cowboy called Arizona reined up his horse for a moment and whittled a chew of tobacco off a twisted plug pulled from a vest pocket. He gazed across the bedded-down herd, every animal of which was visible in moonlight so bright it cast shadows.

Wafting through the clear, still air came a tune from Rawhide Robinson, Arizona's partner this shift on night guard.

I'm fur from my sweetheart and she is fur from me,
And when I'll see my sweetheart, I can't say when it 'twill be,
were the words Arizona heard, distant but distinct. He nudged his horse into a lazy walk with a touch of the spurs and strained to hear the next lines.

> *But I love her just the same, no matter where I roam,*
> *And that there girl will wait for me whenever I come*
> *home.*

The mournful tune raised a lump in the cowboy's throat as he and Rawhide Robinson approached one another on their opposing circles.

I've rode the Texas prairies, I've followed the cattle trail,
I've rid a pitching pony till the hair came off his tail, Rawhide crooned as the two passed, gloved hands raised in lazy greeting. And as the distance between them grew, these words trailed in Rawhide Robinson's wake, drifting softly to Arizona's ears:

*I've been to cowboy dances, I've kissed the Texas
   girls,*
*But there ain't none what can compare with my own
   sweetheart's curls.*

The song haunted the Arizona hand's dreams and troubled him all through the next day. So, after supper, he questioned Rawhide Robinson.

"I ain't never heard that song you was singin' last night, Rawhide. Where'd you come by it?"

"That tune was given to me by an old cowboy in Denver, Colorado, who said it was given to him by a man from Taos, New Mexico, who heard from an old drover out of Waco, Texas, who was said to have got it on a trail drive from an old, stove-up wrangler from down Del Rio way. Where that man got it, I wasn't told. Or, if I was, I lost the thread."

"%^@*&!" said McCarty. "You prob'ly just made it up."

"Hush. Wherever it came from, it is a heart-wrenchin' song," Arizona said.

"That it is," Rawhide Robinson agreed.

Along about that time Doak and another cowboy staggered into camp, each dragging an axe and packing a heavy armload of firewood. They dropped the logs in a clattering heap and fell to the ground, each wiping sweat from his forehead with a shirtsleeve.

"I swear," Doak panted. "Them ol' dead trees down in that dry wash is hard as iron."

"Solid rock, I'd say," said the other cowboy.

"Harder'n any wood I ever put an axe to," Doak said.

Rawhide Robinson said, "You know, boys, that reminds me of something I seen one time—"

"Oh, &#╤@$! Not again!"

"There was this one time, Arizona, when I was down in your country, somewhere up in the northeastern end of the Territory, out near the Painted Desert. You boys ever hear tell of that place?"

"Can't say as I have," one cowboy said.

"No, sir, I don't believe so," said another.

"Ain't no such ^&@#+ place," McCarty said.

"Sure there is," Arizona said. "Ain't seen it, but I've heard about it. Out east of my home country, somewhat."

"So have I heard tell of it," Enos said. "So you might just as well shut up and listen, McCarty. So, what about it, Rawhide?"

"Well, I was riding through that country after havin' taken a herd of beeves to an Indian agent out that way. A hangabout there at the Agency told me about that Painted Desert, and not having anything else on at the time, I figured I'd just as well ride out that way and have a look-see.

"I'll tell you, fellows, that place is every bit as pretty as they say it is. Barren and desolate and dry as salted peanuts, but beautiful all the same. The sand and dirt and rocks come in most every color you can imagine. There's red and orange, yellow and ochre—"

"O what?" McCarty said.

"Ochre. It's a color."

"What color?"

"Well, it's ochre. Sort of light brown, but kind of yellow. Some hint of orange. A little rusty, maybe. It's ochre, is what it is."

"Hah! Just another one of your fancy &^#)@ words, you ask me."

Enos said, "Nobody asked you, McCarty. C'mon, Rawhide, talk on."

"So, anyway, besides ochre and them other colors I mentioned, that desert's got strips and stripes and splashes and splotches of green and bluish colors, too, and more shades of dun than horses come in. Blacks and dark colors, also, and places white as snow.

"I was riding along out there, just admirin' the scenery, and decided to set a spell and give my horse a blow. I come up on this rise and there was this big old log just a-layin' there. It struck me as strange, there being no trees in sight in any direction, and, I'll tell you boys, you can see a hundred miles out there if you can see a rod.

"But, strange as it may seem, that log was sure enough there, and it looked like as good a place to park my carcass as any. So, I dismounted and took a seat.

"Now, here's the strange thing. That log wasn't a log at all. It was a rock! But—and I'll swear to this on Aunt Hattie's grave—it had to have been a log sometime. It had grain, and bark, even annular rings like any old log you'd saw through.

"Annular? ^&%+@#*!"

"A tree grows a new ring every year, McCarty," Enos said. "Annual, annular. Yearly. Get it? Get on with it, Rawhide."

"Well, I got to lookin' around, and there were more of them stone logs scattered here and there. Big ones, little ones, little short chunks, and others as long as a lasso rope. Some places they were scattered hither and yon, other places they was thick on the ground.

"Trees turned into rocks. I ain't never seen nothin' like it, boys."

Said McCarty, "*&$#@+! What about that tree up by the Black Hills you told us about?"

"Oh, that was altogether different. That big old tree stump they call Devil's Tower *froze* solid. It don't ever get cold enough down in that Painted Desert to freeze much of anything. And there were hundreds, thousands, maybe millions of these trees out there in the sand. Like walkin' through what must have been woods a long time ago, until somebody chopped down all the trees. Can't imagine who.

"Strange thing to think about, though, all them trees out there in the desert that way. Found out a few years later that a bunch of book-learned scientists went out there to take a look, and, sure as you're born, them rocks was real trees a long, long, long time ago. Got turned into rocks when they got buried under water—although I can't figure where that much water would have come from, or where it went. Anyway, when them logs got submerged, that water soaked minerals and such into the wood and when the water went away, them trees had turned into minerals altogether. Called it being 'petrified,' them science folks did."

"#$=<@!" What a lot of nonsense," McCarty said.

"It's the truth. You can go see for yourself. If you don't get yourself lost on the way, that is. They call it the Petrified Forest. Once you get to the Painted Desert, just ask anyone for directions."

"%&@*#!"

"McCarty! Knock it off," Enos said. "Matter of fact, take a walk. And take an axe with you and cut some more firewood."

"Careful you don't bust that axe," Doak said. "That wood down there is hard as rocks."

"*$#@+!"

CHAPTER TWENTY-TWO

In which Rawhide Robinson takes the train

With Dodge City drawing ever nearer, the restlessness of the cowboy crew grew palpable. Campfire conversation regularly turned to future plans as the hands contemplated returning to a life they had been apart from these past months—a life that offered views of something other than the backsides of cattle, a seemingly endless sea of horns, and an ever-present cloud of dust.

Being young and barely more than a button and this being his first herd, McCarty grew uncertain in the waning days on the trail.

"So what happens once we get these *&#@(+ beeves to where we're goin'?"

"Whaddya mean, McCarty?"

"Well, I guess I don't know. I mean, I reckon somebody's bought these cattle, or is goin' to. What do we do then?"

Doak chuckled. "The ordinary thing is for us to get paid cash money once the herd's delivered, then ride on into Dodge City and blow it all in a night or two of unbridled revelry."

"Then," Arizona said, "The cook and whatever men Enos can talk into it, or those as wants to, heads south with the chuckwagon and remuda. Me, I'm for takin' the train east, gettin' on a riverboat to New Orleans, then a steamer for Galveston or Brownsville. I'll find me a suitable place to lay around all winter. There, or maybe somewhere over in New Mexico or Arizona where it's warm. Then, I reckon I'll hook up with another herd in the spring and do it all over ag'in."

McCarty screwed up his face, lips twisted and forehead furrowed, changing the contours and creases from time to time as he squatted before the fire, shifting his weight from foot to foot.

"Somethin' botherin' you, kid?" someone asked.

The boy did not answer for a moment. Finally, "You say I could maybe ride on a train?"

"Sure, if you've a mind to," Doak offered. "Why?"

"Well," he said as he squirmed. "I ain't never rid no &^@=!$ train. Fact is, I ain't never even seen one. What're they like, anyhow?"

A chorus of laughter rose from the cowboys and McCarty's face showed more red than the campfire's glow could account for. ")%#*?@!" he muttered, pulling the brim of his hat lower over his face.

"Now, boys," Rawhide Robinson said. "Go easy on the kid. You all had to see your first train sometime, and I don't suppose you knew any more about it then than McCarty knows now. Tell the boy what he wants to know."

The men collected their thoughts for a moment.

"You know," Enos said, "the thing that surprised me most when first I saw a train was how far the darned thing stretched. I knew they strung cars together behind an engine and dragged them along, but I guess I figured it might be three or four of 'em. I never imagined they could line out a dozen, maybe even two dozen, cars. Maybe more."

Doak said, "I never expected all the racket. Them big ol' locomotives huff and chuff even when they's standin' still. Then they spit out steam and it hisses like a herd of barnyard geese. And they got this big brass bell they clang now and then. And, land sakes, when they blowed that whistle I liked to have soiled my trousers."

"I first seen one from a distance, goin' across the prairie," Enos said. "It stretched out along there quite a ways. Like I said, it was a lot longer than I thought one would be. If'n you had to get from one end to the other, it would be far enough you'd want to do it horseback. Too durn far to walk, I'll tell you."

"Once they get to movin' the racket gets worser," Doak said. "The puffing gets louder and when that train driver—"

"—He ain't a driver, he's an engineer."

"—Hush up. Anyways, when that 'engineer' puts the whip to it, the wheels on that engine start in to spinnin' and screechin' and the steam starts spittin' and there's all this crashin' and bangin' as it starts to movin' each car, in turn. See, they don't all start goin' just at once—every car gets jerked by the one in front, and that's how it gets to movin'. Had to cover my ears, I did, to try to drown out all that racket."

"Way down at the other end, after the coal car and all the passenger coaches and baggage car and cattle cars and freight cars and such, there's a car they call a caboose," Enos said. "There's a man who rides back there, sometimes sits in a little box-like deal that sets up on the roof with windows all around. I guess it's his job to see if anything falls off the train. Don't know what good it would do, though, on account of them trains is so long that that feller in the caboose couldn't no way holler loud enough so that the feller drivin' the train could hear him."

"He wouldn't be able to hear him over all that racket, anyhow," Doak said.

McCarty sat wide-eyed, his stare fixated in turn on Enos then Doak then Enos then Doak as they spun their tales. A rare contribution from Arizona shifted his gaze.

Said he, "The smoke is what got to me. Them locomotives—that's the proper name for the business end of the train—spew more smoke than a prairie fire, and it's black as coal. Stinks, too. Burns your eyes. And it's all filled with little bits of ash and cinders that get in your nose and your throat and cover all your clothes till you're as filthy as if you been ridin' drag in the dust for thirteen days straight without crossin' a single stream. Besides being dirty, sometimes them cinders is still hot and'll burn tiny holes in your clothes, or make little brand marks on your hide."

Enos jumped back in and said, "And even long as them trains are, that cloud o' smoke and ash can stretch along behind them even longer."

"At least that smoke don't make no noise," Doak said. "You gotta say that for it. It's quiet, leastways. Not like the clackin' of them wheels ag'in the rails as you go along. 'Course some passenger is apt to let out a yelp now and then if one of them hot ashes burns him."

"$%@-<!" McCarty finally said with a lengthy exhalation of long-held breath. "I can't imagine folks climbin' aboard such an infernal machine on purpose."

"That's just 'cause you ain't never rid one," Doak said. "It's a wonder, it surely is."

"It ain't like ridin' no horse," Arizona said. "Y'know how when you ride, you sort of rock back and forth as the pony goes along? Well, with them trains, you get to swayin' side to side. 'Course that's after you like to get jerked through the back of your seat when it starts out."

" 'Less you're a-sittin' backwards. If you're sittin' facin' backwards when the train starts forwards, why it nearly spills you off the front end of that backward seat," Doak said.

"Backwards? Why, that sounds like a lot of ^@)(*$& nonsense!"

"Watch your mouth, kid," Doak said. "This ain't Rawhide Robinson you're a-talkin' to."

"Say, Rawhide, you been pretty quiet. Ain't you got no train-related adventures?" someone asked.

"Why, sure I do," he said, lost in thought and stretching his chin between thumb and fingers, as if loosening it up for a bout of wagging. "But you boys go on ahead. I'll pitch in later."

"Once you get used to all the jerkin' and rattlin' and smoke and soot and such, it makes for quite a ride," Doak said. "It's a bit unsettling, goin' that fast, at first. You get to wonderin' if it won't upset your constitution permanent-like, goin' that fast—it sure enough can upset your stomach. But there don't seem to be no ill effects that last."

"Them trains hurry along, for sure," Enos said. "They go so durned fast that you can't hardly make out anything that's up close on the outside. Things near the tracks whip past in such a blur you can't rightly see them proper-like. Things farther away, of course, look more ordinary, but even then you pass them by before you hardly notice them."

"^$@_(/*" McCarty said. "I may just go home a-horseback. Don't know if them trains will be to my liking. Guess I'll just have to wait and see, make up my mind once I've laid eyes on one of them things . . ." he said, his voice trailing off into his own thoughts.

Enos let the silence settle in for a while, then asked Rawhide Robinson to tell his tale.

"When I first went up the trail, trains were still just a-makin' their way across the prairies. Every so often a town would sprout where the train was goin' or where it was. Most all them towns in Kansas weren't even there before the railroads come along.

"So, anyway, them capitalist fellows with all the money was always tryin' to outfox one another. They was speculatin' on land—"

"—Spec-u-what-in'?" McCarty interrupted. "What the (&#=>% does that mean? Talk normal."

"Hush," Enos said.

Rawhide Robinson considered an explanation. "Them capitalists is always on the lookout to make a buck, so they would try and find out just where the railroad would be goin' then pick out a likely lookin' spot and buy up all the land thereabout. So when the train got there they could turn a hefty profit sellin' town lots and such."

"Never mind that," someone said. "Tell the story."

"As it happens, speculatin' played into my experience one time."

"How's that?"

"Well, the outfit I once come up the trail with was owned by a man name of Buckshot Branagan. Had this ranch down in the Nueces country, with the B-squared brand. When we was wanderin' through the Indian Territory and on into Kansas, he saw he could save time if he didn't have to go so far east to where the trains was. So he got to dickerin' with them railroad folks about runnin' the rails farther west—which, as it happened, they was figurin' to do anyways.

"So, anyhow, ol' Buckshot Branagan, he filled one of them train company folks with so much whiskey that feller's voice started spillin' over, and he wormed out of him what way the railroad was goin' to go. Then he upped and used the money he got for the cattle to buy hisself a patch of land out there where it would be convenient for the herd to meet up with the railroad.

"When we got back to Texas, he sent a wagon train load of posts and lumber and Dutchmen up there to build shippin' pens. Them Germans made a nice layout; planted enough posts and built enough pens and alleys and chutes and such to handle a passel of cattle. Ol' Buckshot Branagan, he figured he'd really make out next trailin' season, chargin' all the drovers a fee to use the pens, gettin' a commission from the cattle buyers for handlin' the stock, and pocketin' a percentage of shippin' costs from the railroad. He was speculatin' in all manner of ways, as you see.

"Anyway, away we went, early next spring—first herd up the trail. Thing was, never mind all Buckshot Branagan's planning, things didn't work out the way he figgered. Leastways, it would not have had he not sent me on ahead to make sure things was all in order for when we got there with the critters."

Rawhide Robinson hoisted himself off his bedroll, scraped the scraps from his supper plate into the fire, and dropped it into the washtub. He took his sweet time moseying to the cook-fire and splashed a fresh load of scalding coffee into his tin cup. Back at the campfire, holding the cup at arm's length in front of him, he squatted straight down onto his bedroll and tucked his legs, one crossed under the other.

The cowboys watched and waited as he blew the steam off his coffee.

"~+&@%# it, Rawhide! Get on with it!"

"Now, McCarty. You just be patient. We got all the time there is."

Rawhide Robinson wriggled and wiggled and fidgeted until he got himself comfortable. He tipped his hat back, slurped up a sip from his mug, took a deep breath. And waited.

The cowboys sat and squirmed, the tension in the air as tight as a catch rope on the neck of a wild mossy-horn steer. "C'mon, Rawhide! +@)#*$!" McCarty hollered, expressing the frustration of all.

"Simmer down, son. Here's the deal. I got to the shippin' pens them Dutchmen had hammered up, and they looked as pretty as a speckled pup. Thing was, there weren't no railroad anywhere in sight."

Again, Rawhide Robinson paused.

And again, anxious cowboys strained necks and eyebrows and ears toward the storyteller like a herd of bucket calves pursuing a milk pail.

After what seemed a hefty slice of eternity, at least to those thus assembled, Rawhide Robinson talked on.

"Now, boys," he said, "I knowed a railroad wasn't the sort of thing you could conceal, so I set off north to find it. And find it I did."

Again, silence.

And again, cowboy brains stretched so tight they quivered.

Just before they snapped, the raconteur continued.

"I came upon the tracks, just as I figgered I would. But they was a good mile and a quarter north of where they was supposed to be, and had already made their way farther west. So I took up the trail—there ain't no easier tracks to follow than them left by a train—and soon enough come upon the working crews puttin' the finishing touches on rails next to a whole new town, so green the lumber was still seepin' sap. And the tracks ended at a layout of shippin' pens every bit as shiny and new as them built by Buckshot Branagan's German boys."

The cowboys groaned in unison.

"It was a sorry sight, all right. It looked as if Buckshot Branagan's investment was all for naught. But me bein' in his employ, and ridin' for the B-squared brand, I couldn't allow no such thing to happen.

"So I rode on into town, ordered up a refreshing beverage at the saloon, listenin' and watchin' to see what I could learn. There was a feller in fancy town duds there, a fistful of suit-coat lapels in each hand, holdin' forth on the bright future of the town—which just happened to be named after him—a name I don't recall, and am not sorry for the forgetfulness. I offered to stand the man to a drink, and we took a seat at a table in the back corner."

Again, Rawhide Robinson paused to sip and slurp and swallow coffee.

And again, cowboy attention strained until sweat beaded foreheads.

"^%#&*!" McCarty said. Murmurs and mutters of agreement rounded the campfire.

"I'm here to tell you boys, words spilled out of that feller like scours from a sick calf. I couldn't get a word in edgewise, if you can imagine such a thing."

On another evening, such a statement from Rawhide Robison would have drawn chuckles. Not tonight. The cowboys waited in overwrought silence.

"It didn't take too many beers before the story poured out of that bloviator. Fact is, he was happy to tell it. Here's the deal. Not long after Buckshot Branagan rode south the year before, this shyster I was talkin' to wormed his way in with the eastern money men that controlled the railroad. Cash changed hands— hands hidden under tables, if you get my drift—and the railroad changed its route. Weren't nothin' more than bribery, plain and simple. That ring of thieves had snookered Buckshot Branagan without him even knowin' it."

Again, Rawhide Robinson paused.

Immediately, McCarty said, "^&!)>@!" and his saddle pals joined in with their own complaints.

"What then?" said one.

"Then what?" said another.

"Well, I gave it some thought and decided on a plan. I mounted up and took up my back trail and rode on beyond where I'd first found the tracks. I figured it would take about two-and-three-eighths miles of rails for this plan to work, so I rode along about that far and found a likely looking spot and waited for a train.

"I ought to have mentioned the horse I was aboard. Most of the mounts in the cavvy, like always on a drive, was scrubby little Spanish mustangs—not that them ain't the best cow horses ever. But, for this trip, I'd saddled up a big ol' steed that was more American horse, born and bred back east in Kentucky or Tennessee or somewheres. Didn't have a lick of cow sense, but he was big and strong and could cover the miles. You boys know the kind of horse I'm talkin' about—"

"—Forget the horse, Rawhide," someone said. "Get on with the story."

Someone else said, "Yeah, tell us what happened."

"@*#&$^!" McCarty said.

"Take it easy, boys," Rawhide said. "Anyway, after a spell I could see a cloud of smoke comin' my way out of the east, then I could hear that locomotive puffin'—I always did think the 'loco' part was appropriate when talkin' about trains. So I checked my saddle cinches, made sure my catch rope was tied off hard and fast to the horn, and shook out a loop of a size that would make John R. Blocker himself jealous. I spurred my horse into a high lope and rode along beside the train, just keepin' pace with the locomotive.

"I cast my twine and it settled over that engine's smokestack pretty as you please. Jerked my slack and veered off just like draggin' a calf to a brandin' fire. When we hit the end of that rope it liked to have jerked my horse into next week. But, like I said, he was a big, stout animal and he leaned into it and kept scratchin'. Pretty soon, that locomotive started comin' our way, draggin' tracks and train along with it.

"You shoulda seen it, boys! Railroad spikes poppin' like percussion caps in a campfire. Rails bending and twisting and screaming, ties scrapin' and slidin', and the whole layout comin' to heel pretty as you please."

"Well I'll be!" said one surprised cowboy.

"Son of a gun!" said another.

"&^@#*!" said McCarty.

"I kept that rope taut and dragged that locomotive—train,

railroad, and all—across the prairie and lined it out right past Buckshot Branagan's shipping pens, just like nature intended.

"Next day, the B-squared herd showed up, leadin' a whole string of others on the trail behind 'em. The cattle buyers showed up, and overnight a whole town sprung up right there. Ol' Buckshot Branagan wanted to name the place 'Rawhide' in my honor, but modesty forbad me from allowing such a vanity where yours truly is concerned. I wasn't doin' anything more than ridin' for the brand, and deserved no such recognition."

"@?<%#!" McCarty said, slapping his broad-brimmed hat to the ground. "That ain't nothin' more than your usual load of twaddle!"

A wave of laughter rippled out from the campfire, whether spurred on by Rawhide's tale or McCarty's frustration one cannot say.

Someone did say, "Rawhide, is that your only encounter with trains?"

Rawhide Robinson stroked his chin between thumb and fingers, as if calling up another tale.

"Not by a long shot, fellers. I seen somethin' one time that I didn't believe, even while I was lookin' at it—well, at the aftermath of it, I should say."

"Tell us about it!" several voices said in chorus.

But Rawhide Robinson stretched out on his bed, pulled off his boots, and rearranged his saddle from backrest to pillow.

"Not tonight, boys. I'm needin' to check my eyelids for leaks. Some other time."

"Aw, c'mon," someone said.

"Spill it," said another.

"(@+}*#!" said McCarty.

Under his hat, out of sight of his saddle pals, Rawhide Robinson smiled and shut his eyes and was soon washed away on a tide of blissful sleep.

CHAPTER TWENTY-THREE

In which Rawhide Robinson sees a train take a spin

Stinging winds and low-hanging afternoon clouds made for a hard time bedding down the nervous herd, so it was a saddle-weary crew that inhaled a late supper. But the storm passed without breaking and stars stippled the sky till it looked like the hide of a blue roan colt. The campfire snapped, crackled, and popped, sending stars of its own skyward. Heavy-lidded cowhands huddled close, seeking warmth more for its soothing effect than to ward off cold. After a round of coffee and a "man-at-the-pot" refill all around, Doak cleared his throat.

"Rawhide," he said. "What's this you was gonna tell us about a train, but delayed the tellin' in favor of your beauty sleep? Which didn't work, I might add."

"Never mind," McCarty said. "I, for one, ain't in the mood for no more ^%#@* nonsense."

"Aw, kid, give it a rest," came the voice of a cowboy from the other side of the campfire. "Rawhide's tales are always good for a grin, and I sleep better when I'm in a pleasant mood."

"@!?/>=+*!"

"Shut up, McCarty. Tell it, Rawhide."

Rawhide Robinson long-swallowed his coffee and tossed the dregs into the fire with a hiss and wisp of steam. "Here's how it happened," he said.

"See boys, when the railroads first came onto the prairies, it downright aggravated the Indians livin' there. They had no idea what to make of the tracks or the trains or any of it. As you can imagine, them locomotives like to have scared 'em plumb to death. Called it the 'iron horse' for want of somethin' better. Thought all the smoke and clamor was made by evil spirits.

"So it ought not be a surprise that them Indians would retaliate. Which they did. They burned up building supplies and such, but the railroad shipped out more. They tried drivin' off the construction crews, but the army came out to protect them. So they decided to attack the trains themselves. Which ain't no small job.

"The best idea they come up with was tearin' out sections of rails, which would cause trains to derail and crash. Made more'n one mess thataway. When the railroads caught onto that, and sent out track hands to watch out for missing rails, them Indians figured out they could build a fire on the tracks and heat up the rails, then bend 'em this way and that a little, or spread 'em apart just enough to where the wheels of the train would drop through, and they'd crash the train thataway."

"^@?#*&!" said McCarty. "What's all that got to do with anything?"

"Pipe down, kid," someone said. "Let the man tell his story."

"Well, leastways he could get on with it—quit jabberin' on 'bout Indians."

Rawhide Robinson said, "Stay calm, McCarty. It's about to get good."

"?<~*&#!"

"Anyhow, them Indians got downright creative with the games they was playin' with the trains. They figured out the schedules and decided to upset an eastbound night train. So they built bonfires all along about a furlong of track and got them rails as red hot as a blacksmith's horseshoe. And just as malleable."

"Molly who? What the &=+@^# you talkin' about, you old blowhard?"

"Not Molly nobody, McCarty. Malleable. It's an ordinary, everyday word in the English language that means 'capable of being shaped or formed, as by hammering or pressure.' "

"*%(>$!"

"So, anyway, somehow them Indians bent them hot rails up and around in a big ol' loop. Came back around on itself till it almost touched—just barely enough room for the train to fit underneath of the end of the loop, see. So, that night train came smokin' and steamin' down the track full speed ahead and hit that loop and sailed around it like a seed pea rollin' around the bottom of a peach can."

"Well, I'll be!" someone said.

"Who'd a thunk it?" someone else said.

"<!>:&@#}!" McCarty said.

Rawhide Robinson said, "That ain't the half of it. It just so happened the circumference—don't ask, McCarty; circumference means how big around a circle is—of the loop was equal to the length of that train. So the locomotive came around and latched onto the rear end of the caboose and got stuck there. So that train just kept pullin' and pushin' itself around and around that loop.

"Imagine my surprise when I rode over a rise one morning whilst scoutin' for a trail herd, and seein' that train doin' loop-the-loops out in the middle of the prairie."

"That would be some surprise," someone said.

Said Rawhide Robinson, "That it was, boys, that it was. But that still ain't the half of it. We delivered that herd in Ogallala, Nebraska, and when we came back that way—must have been a fortnight or more later—there was that train, still goin' around and around."

">{%@#*!" said McCarty.

"What?"

"I maybe ain't never seen no train, but I ain't so dumb that I don't know they can only go so far before they run out of steam or water or coal, one; all three, maybe even. Then, by =^&@?*, the thing's gotta stop."

"You're right, as far as you go, kid," Rawhide Robinson said. "But here's the thing. Them trains use up fuel and water accordin' to established formulae based on, among other things, distance traveled."

"Huh? That ain't nothing but more of your $%&@}# fancy talk. I ain't got no idea what you're talkin' about."

"Well, McCarty, it's simple. The more country a train covers, the more steam—and the coal and water it takes to make that steam—it uses up. But that particular train, see, going around and around that loop like it was, wasn't coverin' any distance to speak of—wasn't gettin' anyplace at all, therefore it would not have been usin' hardly any fuel or steam at all. So, it just kept on a-goin', goin' nowhere. Could be goin' still, for all I know. Might could go on durn near forever."

">@+$%#," McCarty said. But the tone of his voice betrayed uncertainty. The silence of the others around the campfire likewise indicated an uncommon depth of thought and puzzlement and consideration.

Then again, maybe they were just tired.

CHAPTER TWENTY-FOUR

In which Rawhide Robinson rides away

This evening's sky seemed wider than usual. A faint sundown glow smudged the western horizon while vivid stars poked sharp holes in the already dark dome overhead. Supper dishes soaked in the washtub and the cowboys sat around a crackling campfire, legs radiating outward from the warmth like wagon-wheel spokes.

The campfire—the last the crew would share—lay in a sheltered low place just a few miles south of Dodge City. Trail Boss Enos Atkins had already visited the town and finalized the contract with the cattle buyers; come morning he would go back to town and return with saddle bags heavy with cash to pay off the drovers.

Talk, of course, turned to money and what the cowboys intended to do with their hard-earned, newfound wealth. Celebrations in Dodge City saloons, pleasure houses, restaurants, and haberdashery shops would likely take the largest share. Some talked of sending sums home to struggling families, others vowed to set aside savings for a rainy day, a few contemplated investments in land or livestock.

"How about you, Rawhide?" Enos asked. "Where will your money go?"

"Oh, I don't know. Money don't mean much to me. I've been poor and been rich, been through times both fat and lean, I've lived hard and I've lived soft, and don't see much difference when lookin' back on it."

"Rich?" McCarty said. "&#$%+@! When you ever been rich?"

"Well, not all that long ago, as it happens. Just last fall, I had so much money I could have burned it like autumn leaves. Came into a king's ransom, I did—two of them as a matter of fact."

"Whaddya mean?" Doak wondered.

"You boys recall me tellin' you about that royal family from Eurostandovialand I hired on to guide that one time?"

"Yes," said a chorus of voices.

"And I told you about gettin' them people in the Sandwich Islands started in the cattle-ranching business?

Again, "Yes."

"Well, unbeknownst to me, the Hawaiian King of the Sandwich Islands and the King of Eurostandovialand saw fit to further reward me for my services with transfers of money to a little bank down in El Paso where I had kept a modest sum on deposit since I was just a pup.

"Anyway, both them kings had added a small fortune apiece to my account, and it had been drawin' interest for years without me even knowin' about it. Added up to a tidy sum, it did, and made me a wealthy man."

"+<#@*%!" said McCarty.

"So what did you do with all that money?"

"Well, you know boys, ever since I was a little shaver, I always dreamed of ownin' me a spread. And now I had the means to make that dream come true. I stopped off at the land office and traded all that money for title to a million or two acres of wide-open spaces. I put every penny I had into land, see, on account of I figured I could chouse enough cattle out of the brasada to stock it, and round up enough wild horses to do the chousing.

"I hired me a crew—a colorful bunch of characters, names of

Jefferson and Nacho and Eagle Beak and Bok Choy—and we headed out to the ranch, which wasn't a ranch as yet, you understand. We looked the place over, then looked it over again, finally deciding on the best location for a headquarters. We didn't even think about puttin' up a house—the most important thing bein' corrals and pens and pastures and such to get us started in the cattle business.

"Punchin' post holes in that caliche was no small job, I'm here to tell you. Every hole we dug took a goodly amount of sweat, and we had a goodly number of post holes to dig. But me and Jefferson and Nacho and Eagle Beak and Bok Choy got it done.

"Thing was, though, after the day we dug the last post hole, we had just bedded down for a good night's sleep when the wind came up. Now, any of you boys as has been to West Texas don't need me to tell you how the wind can blow out there. It blowed and it blowed all the night long.

"Me and Jefferson and Nacho and Eagle Beak and Bok Choy huddled under the wagon the whole night through while that wind whipped around us, and I'll tell you we like to been sanded smooth from all the grit in the air. We was all spittin' mud pies, for sure.

"Come sun-up, we scraped all the dirt and rocks out from under our eyelids and took a look around. I could have cried. Fact is, boys—and I am not ashamed to admit it—I did cry. Bawled like a newborn baby that's just been smacked on the backside.

"And you would have cried too, I daresay, if you saw what me and Jefferson and Nacho and Eagle Beak and Bok Choy saw. When the sun went down I had been a budding cattle baron. When the sun came up, circumstances had once again placed me firmly among the penniless."

Some of the boys around the campfire that evening swear to

this day that they saw Rawhide Robinson wipe away a tear. Others hold that he was merely rubbing tired eyes, as the hour was late and the time for reasonable drovers to be asleep had long since passed. In any event, it took a few minutes for the man to collect himself and carry on with the story.

In his own good time, Rawhide Robinson again took up the tale.

"You should have seen it, boys. It was a sorry sight. My whole ranch had done gone and blown clean away in all that wind. Every square inch of every acre of my cattle empire had up and relocated to somewhere down in Old Mexico. The whole ranch just peeled up and flew plumb away in a cloud of dust.

"Fact is, the only piece of land left with my name on it was that little patch there under the wagon where me and Jefferson and Nacho and Eagle Beak and Bok Choy had huddled in the windstorm, where, I guess, we held it in place firmly enough to keep it from gusting off with the rest of the ranch.

"I'll tell you, boys, it was so bad there was nary a trace of the place. Why, so much had blowed away that all them post holes me and Jefferson and Nacho and Eagle Beak and Bok Choy had dug down into the ground were now sticking up out of it! Every one of them, poking up all over the place as high as they used to be low!"

"*&@#$%!" McCarty was heard to say.

"Hush up!" several other cowboys said in reply.

"Talk on, Rawhide," someone else said.

"Well, having run plumb out of options, I hitched up the team and drove all around where my ranch headquarters was supposed to be while Jefferson and Nacho and Eagle Beak and Bok Choy cut off all them post holes and stacked them in the wagon. Then we hauled that load of post holes into town, where I sold them all to the dry goods store there.

"See, I convinced the storekeep that since they were brand

new and in good shape, he wouldn't have much trouble shiftin' them to sodbusters and other settlers coming into the country. Seein' as how I was in a fix, he also took the team and wagon off my hands.

"Every penny them post holes and wagon outfit brought was just barely enough to cover wages for Jefferson and Nacho and Eagle Beak and Bok Choy.

"And that left me with nothin' to my name but a saddle and the horse under it. I rode the grub line for a while, just wanderin' from ranch to ranch, wallowing in ennui and sufferin' from a severe bout of depression. Then I run into you all boys gathering up this herd, and asked Enos to sign me on as a trail hand.

"You boys know the rest."

Even McCarty was subdued by the gloomy mood resulting from Rawhide Robinson's tale. No comment or conversation ensued, and soon the sound of snoring accompanied the crackling fire and bubbling coffee pot.

Sunrise brought a crew of mounted cowboys riding out from town. Hired by the new owners of the cattle, they circled the herd and lined it out toward the shipping pens at the railyard. For the first time in more than 1,500 miles the cattle moved unaccompanied by Enos Atkins's hired hands.

Just as the dust settled and the last steer's tail disappeared over the low rise north of camp, Enos came galloping into camp and finished off with a showy sliding stop.

"Here it is, boys! You've earned it, now come and get it!"

Enos sat upon a water keg and used the drop table at the end of the chuckwagon to count out the cash. The cowboys stood patiently in single file, some with faint smiles, others with silly grins, as their trail boss counted out stacks of gold coins.

"I can almost taste that first mug of beer," Arizona said.

"I can almost taste a fried egg. Maybe a dozen of them," Doak said.

"@#$%&! I can almost smell that sweet perfume," McCarty said, then blushed from the collar of his shirt to the brim of his hat.

Once all were paid off, saddled up, and ready to go, the cowboys congregated for the ride to town, organized into small groups according to interests—this one bound for a saloon, that one for an eating house, those for the telegraph office, these for the parlor houses.

"How 'bout you, Rawhide? You comin' with us?"

"No, boys, I don't believe so."

"C'mon, Rawhide, ride along with us."

"Thanks just the same, Doak, but I don't believe I will."

"I suppose you can come with us, you ol' #$%*@."

"No, McCarty. That's a sport for a younger man."

Rawhide Robinson shook hands with each of his erstwhile saddle pals, turned tail to Dodge City, and rode off at a restrained gallop, twirling a loop just for fun and whistling a happy tune.

EPILOGUE

The meals in the bunkhouse were good. That was one thing. An outfit with a good cook was a good find for a wandering cowhand.

This night, the board held biscuits as well as yeast rolls, beans seasoned with bacon and chili peppers, beefsteaks with gravy, spuds fried with onions, carrots boiled with raw sugar, rice pudding with raisins, and sweet buttermilk.

And, of course, an unlimited supply of hot coffee.

After supper, the hands wandered into the sleeping room. Some plopped onto their cots and took up handwork such as repairing headstalls, adjusting spur straps, and stitching saddlebags; more for want of involvement than out of necessity. Others thumbed through well-worn books and tattered magazines with a decided lack of interest. A few sat around a small round table on mismatched chairs and pretended interest in the cards dealt them.

Soon enough, yawns started and more than one cowboy warded off the sandman by grinding fists into itchy eyes, while others stretched arms and shoulders with fists raised and elbows wide. But the sleepiness came not from fatigue; it was merely a physical manifestation of boredom. What was wanted was something—a song, a story, a poem, a recitation—to cut through the tedium, entertain, and engage the minds of the off-duty cowboys.

Among the men in the bunkhouse was a cowboy of late

middle age, a holdover from the end of the great trail-driving days. He was a quiet man, and for the few weeks since wandering onto the ranch and hiring on, he had gone about his job in a businesslike manner, worked hard, and said little.

And so it was that none of the other hands felt they really knew the new man. Few even remembered his name. It's not that they did not like him, for it was simply impossible to dislike such a capable cowboy. Still, no one had established any kind of bond with the quiet old cowhand.

And so it was that a certain amount of surprise permeated the bunkhouse when the itinerant cowboy—whose name was McCarty, by the way—spoke.

"Say, any of you boys ever come across an old cowboy name of Rawhide Robinson?"

A wave of headshakes rippled around the bunkhouse, interrupted by the occasional spoken, "No."

"Well, I knew him. Went up the trail with him one time. Quite the trip, it was. Enough &^@~# adventures to last a lifetime. Anyway, there was this cowboy name of Rawhide Robinson along. Older fellow, he was—seemed to me ancient at the time, but he was years younger than what I am now, I suppose.

"You'd have to say he was ordinary in every regard. Wasn't nothin' extra to look at. Not too tall, not what you'd call handsome. Average kind of horseman, handy with a rope but not exceptionally so."

All trace of lassitude left the bunkhouse and each and every cowboy was totally engaged in what McCarty said.

"Thing was, the most extraordinary things happened to this ordinary cowboy. Some of his &@#*$% adventures defy belief. Still and all, they're all true.

"Why, boys, let me tell you; there was this one time when ol' Rawhide Robinson . . ."

ABOUT THE AUTHOR

Two-time winner of the coveted Western Writers of America Spur Award, **Rod Miller** is a versatile writer. His books include fiction, history, and poetry; his short stories and poems appear in several anthologies; and he writes for Western magazines. He is a member of Western Writers of America. *Rawhide Robinson Rides the Range* is Miller's first novel for Five Star. Visit his website at *www.writerRodMiller.com.*